BONDAGE BITES

69 SUPER-SHORT STORIES
OF LOVE, LUST AND BDSM

EDITED BY
ALISON TYLER

CLEIS
PRESS

Published in the United States by Cleis Press, an imprint of Start Midnight, LLC, 101 Hudson Street, Thirty-Seventh Floor, Suite 3705, Jersey City, New Jersey, 07302.

Cover design: Scott Idleman/Blink
Cover photograph: iStockphoto
Text design: Frank Wiedemann

First Edition.
10 9 8 7 6 5 4 3 2 1

Trade paper ISBN: 978-1-62778-118-3
E-book ISBN: E-book ISBN: 978-1-62778-134-3

Love is the master key which opens the gates of happiness.
—Oliver Wendell Holmes

If one is master of one thing and understands one thing well, one has at the same time, insight into and understanding of many things.
—Vincent van Gogh

Contents

INTRODUCTION

Why bondage?

For me, that's like asking, Why food? Why air? Why sleep (however little of it I manage)? But some people wonder. Why does your heart beat faster for kink? Why would you want to tie someone down? Why would you want to be bound?

Oh, sweet heaven, *because*.

Because of everything that goes with the word *bondage*. Start with the implements: the cuffs, the ties, the silk, the rope, the hardware, the software, the chains, the collars, the leather. A true bondage fiend can get aroused by the gear alone.

Next let's discuss the vocabulary. Bondage has its own language, its own rules and regulations. Even beyond that there's the rhythm, the very cadence, the poetry, if you will: *Yes, Sir. No, Sir. On your knees, boy. Up against that wall, doll. Did I say to look at me? Did I say that you could stand? Bow down. Count. Do I stutter? No, Mistress. Yes, Ma'am. Whatever you want. Whatever you say.*

And then we have the outfits. Sure, you can be into bondage with a stark-naked closet. But why? We have short skirts, tight pants, high-heeled boots, leather, PVC, rubber, masks, costumes. Fashion is often inspired by bondage and not the other way around. Check your latest *Vogue* if you don't believe me.

But in my world, the most important part of bondage is the thousand-watt charge of power—the electricity you feel between two (oh yes, or more) lovers. You ask for what you want and someone fulfills your need. Or you don't even have to ask. Your partner simply knows. This connection doesn't exist for me in vanilla sex. The power of bondage can be as pure as a command to hold still, or a pair of hands on a lover's wrists, an emotional bond. Players can move up the ladder to the extreme sensations—but everything begins with that flickering glow of power.

In this book, the stories capture that current. From emotional bondage to full-scale dungeon scenarios, these stories delve deep into the passion of this much-loved genre. The pieces are short—some only one hundred words—but each one is lit up, bright as neon on a midnight sky.

Why bondage?
Because I can't fucking breathe without it.

XXX,
Alison

B

Alison Tyler

Don't keep me in your back pocket, tucked into your battered leather wallet, behind the ticket stub for the movie we went to see. Don't tell yourself you don't need me, that you can get by with the grown-up cheerleaders, the girls who twirl their curls over drinks, the ones who wait for you to open the car door, who think it's not a date unless the man pays.

Don't pretend that what we did has no meaning. That the way you held my arms over my head hasn't resonated inside of you.

I call foul.

But I have time.

Take her out, the next one, the next sweet young thing. Take her out to the latest restaurant written up by some pompous blowhard in the local paper. Watch her toy with her food. Watch her play with her hair.

Take her home and stand on the front porch beneath the safety light and kiss her good night with the paper-fine moths fluttering manically over your head. Know that she is calculating exactly how many dates you're going to pay for before she lets you in, before she pours you a drink, before she spreads her legs.

Go on home, man. Take out that ticket stub, run the ball of your thumb along the edge, close your eyes and remember.

I had on a black jersey skirt, short, just above the knee. Black T-shirt, cut tight, showing everything I have to show—compact body, high small breasts. I was wearing tights that he'd already ripped once, high up under the hem. You couldn't see the hole at first, but I felt the breeze. My purse was a simple leather pocket on a thin leather strap. Docs completed the look, tied tight to the knee. I don't wear much makeup. My face was bare except for dark lipstick, black mascara. In the flicker of the foreign film, you kept looking at me.

I walked out in the middle. You followed me. I headed upstairs to the ladies. You didn't hesitate. We entered together, and I said, "So you haven't done this before."

You shook your head.

The pretty blonde chicklets don't let you do this to them? They don't let you cuff them in a bathroom and fuck them against the wall?

I'd told you exactly what I wanted, exactly what I

needed. I'd told you that if you met my specifications I would walk past you down the aisle. I'd told you to bring the cuffs and the key. I'd signed the mail with my safeword.

Why would I trust a novice dom?

Because I sensed you'd be eager to give me the moon.

You had my arms over my head, pulling me to my full height. You kissed me, and I could feel your hard-on against your jeans. You said, "Why do you want this?" and I said, "You don't get to know that yet."

You dragged me to the last stall, cuffed my wrists, pushed me up against the cold plaster. You slid my skirt to my waist, stroked my ass through the stockings, let one firm slap land on my ripe cheeks. The sweet spot.

You said, "What does bondage do for you?"

And I said, "You don't get to know that yet."

"When?"

"When you prove your worth."

You had my stockings down, torn farther in your strong hands. You had my panties down, too, and you spanked me until my ass felt swollen. It had been too long. I stared at the graffiti scrawled on the wall—JOHN LOVES JANE 1972—and I steeled myself and I thought of him and I thought of you and I almost came. You ground your hips against me, your clothed cock against my naked split, and you said, "I want to take you somewhere. Somewhere else."

I shook my head. Not yet. Just this.

You spread my legs. You let your fingers spank my cunt. And I came. Fiercely, silently. I came on your fingertips and then you brought your hand to my mouth and I licked the juices—my juices—away.

You split your jeans, opened a condom. I could hear the crackle, the rustle of the Mylar. Sheathed, you slid into my pussy, so wet, so ready for you. I set my forearms against the wall. I rested my forehead on the cold tile. I accepted the force of you, brutal, powerful, your thrusts rhythmic. Like poetry.

When you came, you bent to bite my shoulder through my T-shirt. I wore your teeth marks home that night.

You undid the cuffs, you set me free. I left the stall and waited for you.

"Do you have your ticket?" I asked.

"I need a ticket to ride the ride?"

I waited. You handed it over. I dug in my bag for a pen and I wrote my number on the edge.

"When you're ready for what comes next," I said. "When you're sure about what you want."

—B

DANGER

Sommer Marsden

I liked the danger of it. I liked the thrill. It was Teddy who jokingly said I should let him put me in his display. That was after a drunken night out on the town. One too many sips of pink Moscato and one too many confessions.

It's how I found myself bound to a telephone pole in his Halloween display. Luckily it wasn't too cold and I had time alone—just bound there half-nude and thinking—to contemplate if I wanted to go through with my little exhibitionist's dream come true. One breast was artfully exposed. And my pussy was barely covered in what looked to be old dirty rags, but were actually pieces of linen we'd stained with tea to give them that aged look. I was set up to look like the damsel in distress. The waif. The girl held captive by the monster. I was Fay

Wray on display.

I thought about it a thousand times in the course of the twenty minutes before he opened the gate. Wondered if I should leave. If this was a bad idea. Considered that I was quite possibly insane. And yet every time I opened my mouth to call out to Teddy to ask him to let me loose, I quickly silenced myself. I shut my eyes and simply listened. To my pounding heart. To the pulse of my body. And I let myself focus on how wet—no, how *drenched*—I was between my thighs.

And I shut my mouth.

The first wave of people didn't seem to notice anything off with me. I kept my breath shallow. My body still. I hung my head as if dejected but mostly it was to keep in character and to cover my face. I watched the parade of people who sought fear and titillation, and I tried not to react to the starburst of excitement that detonated beneath my skin, thrilling me to the core.

The second wave was different though. As I studied them, a man studied me back. A tall, thick man with forearms the size of my thighs. His dark hair was shaggy and his blue eyes were bright. Interested. I felt my pulse skip erratically, felt my head go muzzy and light from holding my breath. Under his gaze my knees dipped just a little. Imperceptibly really.

But he smiled.

Caught.

The rush it gave me was like no other. The rush it

gave me was intoxicating.

I exhaled, disappointed, when he continued on down the line.

My shoulders ached, my back, too. I'd been clenching my jaw and the tension radiated down my neck and up into my temples. I wanted so badly to shift and had to control the instinct. I was focused on the piercing ache right between my shoulder blades when I felt someone loosen the ropes.

I gasped, thinking it had to be Teddy. Until an unfamiliar gruff voice rasped in my ear. "I'm here to save you, Pretty. Did you think I wouldn't notice you breathing? It was hard." He chuckled then at his double entendre. "But I noticed. I'm a hunter. We're trained to be observant."

I realized I should fight. Deny him. Maybe call out for Teddy. Very few people paid attention to the giant man untying me and scooping me up in his arms. Most probably assumed it was part of the Halloween display. I didn't know him. He was a stranger. And yet…

Arousal swept me under, filled every cell in my body. Made me go limp in his arms.

"Good girl."

He smelled good. Soap and clean cotton and some subtle spicy cologne. His arms were huge. His beard tickled my forehead where it touched me. He carried me to a greenhouse that was dark and closed—not part of the event.

He set me on a potting bench and parted my thighs.

His fingers, as if by magic, found my wetness and he let loose another low laugh. "Should I introduce myself?"

I shook my head. No. That wasn't what this was. This was…a craving.

The danger and the rush and the fear were all part of the turn-on.

I relaxed under his touch, wondering if I should, not caring. I shuddered when he stroked my clit again. Sighed loudly when he slipped a thick finger inside me.

"You're a good heroine. Very convincing. I wanted to save you the moment I saw you," he said, pinching my bare nipple and then baring the other one so they matched.

His mouth was hot, his facial hair perfectly harsh. Goose bumps pebbled my breasts where his beard rasped.

As he sucked he slid another finger inside me, then added a second. He burrowed both fingers deep inside me, curling them gently at first, and then fucking me roughly with them. My body gripped him tight and pleasure swept me along. Heat and wetness unfurled inside me and I arched my hips up on the rickety potting bench, hearing it groan even as I came with a stifled cry.

In the semidarkness, I heard his zipper perfectly clearly. The evening chill was setting in and a smell tremble had started deep in my bones. He smoothed my hair back, tsking roughly. When he grabbed my hips and hauled me forward so my ass was on the lip of the bench, I gasped.

Big hands parted my thighs farther, held my thighs as if supporting my body was no effort at all. His cock, hot and hard, slid the length of my nether lips, kissed my clitoris, making me tremble. And then he was in me. One hard thrust. One brutal entry.

He held me stable, fucked me hard, rocking into me so the bench smacked the back wall making the small structure shake. I let myself slip deeper into the fantasy. Gave in to the feel of the rescue by the hulking stranger. Allowed myself the sensation of being safe in his grip.

He pressed his hot mouth to my throat, clasping my hips so tightly I imagined red fingerprints remaining there on my flesh for hours. He grunted like some beast and that made it all the better. All the crazier. All the more dangerous.

I felt myself shaking in his grip and he pinched my nipple again, bit my throat gently, slammed into me. I came when his teeth found the tip of my breast, when his cock hit just the right spot, when his fingers pinched a tad too harshly.

I cried out loudly this time and as he chuckled, amused by my loss of control, he pulled free of me, painting my thighs and my belly with his come. It seemed luminescent in the purpling gloom.

"Do you feel safe?" he asked, grinning in the almost dark.

I was too shaken to answer. My entire body was a heartbeat.

"Would you like me to tie you back up?"

I shook my head.

The big man reached into his pocket and took out a card. He tucked it in the small remainder of the tank top that had barely covered my chest. Then he kissed me and turned to go.

"Just in case you want me to save you again," he said.

And then he was gone. I was alone, nearly nude, and in possible peril once again. Just the way I'd always fantasized.

STRIPPED

Stella Harris

G race dresses carefully, choosing each garment with precision, from matching lingerie to the most flattering outfits. She dresses for access and appeal: skirts that can be pulled up around her waist and heels that lengthen her legs. But in the end it doesn't matter.

He tells her to strip and doesn't even watch. What she's wearing isn't relevant; he's interested in what's underneath. And not just her body, he's looking much deeper than that. Sometimes Grace thinks he can see right through her. It's uncanny.

He seems to know that by having her strip she's laid bare, her armor of confidence removed. Grace is instantly vulnerable: to his gaze, to his touch, to his tools and toys and most significantly to his mind and intellect.

It's not his physical strength that holds her, though

he is by far the stronger person. Nor the security of her cuffs or bindings, though they are tight. What holds her still is far more subtle and powerful; she is held by the force of her desire to please him.

The order to strip is the first command of the scene, but it won't be the last. It sets the tone; she is to obey. And she does obey, with an almost frantic eagerness. With every action Grace strives to show just how good she can be for him.

The frenetic energy is all contained within her; outside is calm and quiet while inside thoughts tumble through her mind. Her body screams and thrills at each new sensation, but outside all is silence.

Until it isn't.

Are those sounds coming from her? The gasps, moans and shrieks? The begging voice Grace hardly recognizes as her own?

There's his voice too, calming and centering.

Can she last a little longer?

Can she take a little more?

Can she?

Yes.

Yes.

Yes.

DOLLFACE

Tamsin Flowers

When he had secured the last knot to his satisfaction, Toby stepped back to look at his handiwork. Dollface was lying naked, facedown, on the dining table, her wrists and ankles tied securely to the four table legs at the corners with a soft black rope he'd bought specially for the purpose. It was a big table and her legs were spread wide, allowing Toby to enjoy the view: the black rope against her lily-white skin, the soft pink rose of her vagina, blossoming in the heat.

"You're beautiful, Dollface," Toby said.

Dollface didn't answer, probably because Toby had applied a ball gag to her mouth before he started to tie her up.

None of it was particularly necessary—the ball gag, the ropes. Dollface was a passive creature. She rarely said much and that was one of the reasons why Toby liked her so much. Adored her, in fact. A quiet girl who loved to be restrained as much as he loved to restrain her. They were so well suited.

Toby stroked her back as he walked around the table. Her skin was cool to the touch. Smooth and flawless. It made his cock buck. Time he got out of his pants. He ruffled her hair, so long and soft, like spun gold, and then undid his fly. His pants slid to the floor. He like to get undressed in front of her, where she could see him if she dared look up. But she didn't. Her pleasure was tied to restraint and self-restraint.

Naked now, Toby took a breath and savored the moment. His beautiful girl, waiting silently and throbbing with need. He knew what she wanted. She wanted him to take her, first in her soft pink pussy and then in her tight little ass. She was greedy and she wanted a double dose of fun. But Toby was the man to give it to her. He stroked his cock fondly, his hand appreciating its hardness, his cock responding to the caress with a rush of heat and a dribble of precome.

There was a tube of lube in the top drawer of the dresser; he was always prepared and he wanted to be able to slip in easy without hurting her. He went around to the foot of the table and climbed up on his knees on the small triangle of dark wood between her splayed legs. He lubed his fingers and swept them down into the dark crevice between her legs, eliciting a squeak from Doll-face and a low groan from himself. He leaned forward and swept her hair to one side so he could nuzzle her shoulder and the side of her neck. Her body was soft beneath his, the rise of her buttocks like billowing clouds on the flat plain of the table.

It was time. Supporting himself on his knees and one hand, Toby used his other hand to guide himself into the slick embrace of Dollface's wet pussy. He was enveloped by her and it felt so good. He slipped in and out, pressing down hard against her ass, grinding his hips into her as he plunged deeper. He reached around to squeeze her breast, perfectly round in his hand with a hard nub of nipple.

He twisted it and her body bucked. He rode her harder, grunting with the exertion. He was sweating now, skidding across her back as a slippery sheen built between them. With each push down against her ass, her pussy tightened round him, clenching, holding him and adoring him. He slid a finger down between them to prepare her for his second ingress, spreading her buttocks and stroking lube across the small, sweet pucker. He wanted to come in her ass, fill it with his come, ram hard into her until she had to bite down on the gag and strain against the ropes.

He worked it with his finger till he felt she was ready to take him, then he pushed up against it. It was tight but he knew, with a bit of work, he would fit. And then the heavenly squeeze, the painful grip of her ring of muscles as he thrust in and out. Just feeling the knotty entrance with the tip of his cock was almost enough to make him come, but he wasn't going to let his girl down. He clenched his jaw and fought the sensations as he slowly applied enough pressure to gain entrance. Dollface didn't relax; if anything she clenched even tighter around him and as he thrust in and out he was on that glorious cusp between pain and pleasure, the best feeling in the world, and he knew that she would be feeling it too.

He grappled for her nipple and pulled on it hard as Dollface strained against the ropes at her wrists.

POP!

With a rush of air she deflated and Toby's thrusting dick crashed into the unyielding surface of the table underneath.

"Goddammit!"

It was the third Lovedream DeLuxe Doll he'd burst this week.

CHALK

Kathryn O'Halloran

Put your hands here and here," he says.

I move as he tells me, placing my hands on the iron bed frame. Then I wait. I wait for him to tie me, with ropes or leather or even silk cords. He knows what I want and why I come here.

But instead he gets out a stick of chalk. Chalk? What the fuck? I want to raise my head and ask him but I know better than that.

He rubs the chalk on black iron, a mark each side of my hands and I wonder what this game is.

"Don't move," he says. "If you move your hands, you'll smudge the chalk and I'll know. I'll see the smudges and I'll know."

"But…"

"Silence."

I want to weep. A girl needs something more than chalk.

At first I can hear the birds outside and I can feel the springs in the mattress beneath my knees and the strain in my back. Then my mind plays tricks on me. Did he leave the room or did he stay? I thought I heard him leave but maybe that was last time?

I think I can feel the heat of him hovering very close to my skin at times. I think I can hear the slow creak of a floorboard in the way that someone who is trying not to make a noise would make it creak.

I could raise my head and look around but if I do, I might move my hands without realizing. I might smudge the chalk.

My breathing slows down as I sink down lower into myself. This is how he gets me. How he makes me condense. All feeling, all thought, all distractions are gone.

Then I think of only one thing. If I move my little finger. Not even move it, just raise it up from the post a little; I could do that. He would never know. Even if he is in the room watching, he won't know. All I need to do is raise it and put it down in exactly the same spot.

I think about raising it. I think about the motion. I wonder if my hands have gone white from holding on so long and gripping so tight.

Then I think I feel him again. A ghost of a touch. I shiver. I know he is there, sitting in the chair in the corner quietly watching. And I am here bent over on the bed with my head down and my back slightly bowed and my hands gripping the posts and not moving. Not a muscle. Not a flinch.

But he is not here. I heard him leave. I thought I heard him leave.

I will move my finger, I decide. I will it but my finger doesn't move. My finger obeys when my mind does not and I wonder if I will ever be able to move again.

Then I hear footsteps and the door opening. He returns to the room even though he's always been here and he takes my left hand from the post and he turns it palm up. Then he does the same with my right. The chalk is unsmudged.

UP/DOWN

Vida Bailey

He knows. He knows the words to whisper to lock my hands in place. He knows how to make me freeze and ready myself for the ties. He knows how to bind me so safely and tightly that I can't move at all, how to bend me completely to his whim. And he knows how to take every little bit of choice away, so for once I'll stop thinking, stop analyzing, stop worrying. He knows how to push me so I can fall without fear, openheartedly, so I can come freely in his tightly locked chains.

I know, sweetheart, when you want to you can take it all away. You can bind me tighter and tighter into a space that expands, twist me up into nothing while my fear finds wings. All in the moment, all heartbeat and pulled shoulders, stretched neck. Your hand pulling my hair into a thousand tiny points of pain, mouth stuffed with you, breath gasping, panicking around you. Your hand at my throat and your kiss. You kiss safety. Firm lips pressed to me, I am anchored. Anchored I follow the line back to where you are. I follow the line home.

TAKEN FOR
A RIDE

Tilly Hunter

The trunk of the car. You know it's stupid. You guess it's illegal. And your car is tiny. I mean, it even fits in the garage at your new house. It's the first garage you've owned, but even you know that garages are for storing bicycles and ladders. No one actually parks in them.

But there's the thing. Your tiny car fits in your garage. You can open that tiny trunk in private. Put things in it. In private. Stare at the dimensions. In private. Empty out assorted picnic blankets and wet-weather gear and snow shovels and hiking boots and rest your ass on the plastic rim next to the catch. In private. Lean back nonchalantly, hands going inside onto the scratchy gray carpet, until you can drop your ass inside. In private. And then, well, you're almost all the way. Might as well just see. Swing those legs round, lower your upper body and you're in.

You're lying in the trunk of your city runaround staring out at the metal shutter of the garage door and imagining what it would be like to have someone else put you there. All in private—until your husband appears, having padded round silently from the side door into the utility room.

You blame it on movies. It doesn't matter if they've involved men or women. What matters is that the actor-slash-kidnap victim has her hands tied behind her back. At least. Ankles are optional. Other rope configurations—optional. Tape across the mouth is theatrical but not very practical. A blindfold or hood. That could work. But maybe the point is to realize how dark it is in there when the lid slams down. To blink up in dazzled fear when you hear the click of it opening again and see that first sliver of light as you squirm against your restraints to wedge your body into the farthest corner away from your captors.

"Honey, you seem to be in the trunk." He's not particularly surprised. Which would be odd, in some other relationship. Some vanilla, missionary position on a Friday night relationship. But, thank fuck, you don't have one of those, despite becoming a respectable garage owner.

"Yes, dear, I do. I just thought I'd try it out now that we have the garage. You know."

He knows. He doesn't even give you time for second thoughts, doesn't try to talk sense into you. Instead, he grabs a length of rope—what was it even doing in the garage?—and asks you to turn over so he can bind your wrists behind you. And that's it, you're lost, all sense gone. All senses alive. The chemical scent of cheap upholstery, the scratch of it on your cheek and bare forearms, the taste of rubber and oil in the air as your mouth falls open and your tongue flicks over your lower lip, wishing for a shoulder to lick, an earlobe, the tip of a penis.

"Are you my poor little kidnap victim?" he whispers in your ear, hot breath making your hairs stand up. "Where will I take you? What will I do to you? Will you ever escape?"

You look up at him; your mouth's open but the link between brain and vocal chords has been severed. You breathe that acrid scent of car while he binds your ankles. Where is he getting all this rope from? You keep rope in the bedroom, not the garage.

And then he does it. Slams the lid. And it is dark. If you crane your head round to where the parcel shelf meets the backseat, there's a chink of light at the corners but that's it. Your cunt's starting to throb and you're wondering how long he'll give it before he lets you out and fucks you. Then you hear a rumbling. The garage door going up. The next thing you feel more than hear. Vibrations all along the lower side of your body as the engine fires up and starts pumping waste gases through the pipes beneath you. Newtonian forces fight gravity, rolling your skin and bones against that thin carpet as the car moves backward, swings round and accelerates away. It's at that moment that your brain has a reality check.

"He's actually fucking well driven off with you in the trunk," it says, as if it's disavowing any part in events.

Corners. Braking. Stops. Starts. Rights. Lefts. Those books where the kidnap victim memorizes a route from the movement of the vehicle even though she can't see... It's all bullshit. You're starting to feel a bit sick when there's a longer stop that lets your stomach settle, but not your cunt. Despite the dizziness, your cunt has kept throbbing so much that even the thought of the hot exhaust pipe has become phallic.

Movement again. The nausea holds off. You press your cheek into a bit of grit caught in the nylon fibers beneath your face. It's probably come off the bottom of your hiking boots, some bit of dried-up trail dirt. You're rubbing against it, savoring the itchy discomfort, when the car comes to a more decisive stop and the engine cuts. A door opens. Shuts. The garage door rumbles. A catch clicks and the lid starts to open. The light dazzles you even though the garage door is closed once more.

"Enjoying yourself?"

You make some kind of guttural sound that you hope conveys the meaning, "Fuck me now."

"You'll have to wait," he says. "I got drive-through." He waves the brown paper bag in explanation, before slamming the lid down again.

You almost find your voice. But what comes out is not a word; it's delirious frustration.

SHOWING RESTRAINT

Thomas S. Roche

W hat about these?" asked Paul. He reached over Jasmine's shoulder and plucked another pair of padded leather restraints from the rack. They were considerably heavier than the workaday pair Jasmine held in her hands; these had padding of smooth black material with a faux-fur look.

Paul held the new restraints up for Jasmine to inspect. He still towered over her, his big arm reaching over her shoulder. He held the restraints just a little too close to her face—too close for comfort that is. But she didn't move away.

Instead, she took a deep, deep breath of the new-leather scent. It hit her like a sledgehammer. She swooned. She would have been flattened, just like a character in some cartoon, if Paul's broad body hadn't been right there behind her to prop her up, and if his big hand hadn't been there on her shoulder to steady her.

Paul felt her sway. His fingers, powerful but gentle, closed at that place where her shoulder met her collarbone. As Jasmine took another deep breath, the scent of the leather seemed to suffuse her body. She felt it right down to her core...and beyond, where she felt pretty sure her panties were getting quite wet.

Jasmine never took her sparkling green eyes off the new, heavier restraints in Paul's hand. She just kept staring and breathing deeply. She fumbled the pair she'd been holding back on the metal rack. Paul's hand had lightened up slightly on her shoulder and collarbone. The tips of his fingers had started to work, gently tickling her flesh in a peculiarly sensitive spot only he seemed to have ever been able to find. The other guys she'd been with had kissed her there, caressed her there...it had been fine, but not like *this*. It felt like Paul had some occult knowledge that told him how to find that spot on her neck that simply didn't exist in three dimensions.

He knew other spots, too, farther back, toward the nape of her neck. He worked his way back there, his fingers light and deft, while Jasmine just stared and breathed.

Paul's voice was a susurrant growl in Jasmine's ear.

"Well?" he said.

"I like them," she said. She breathed deep. "God, they smell great."

"Take them," said Paul, as if telling her to go ahead and take a cookie. "Feel the weight."

Jasmine hesitated.

"Um," she said. "How much are they?" The price tag dangled from one buckle, a plain white tag on a string, but it spun in the breeze from the air-conditioning vent. She couldn't tell if that was a five or an eight. And was that a one or a seven?

"Don't worry about it," said Paul. "Take them. What do you think of the *feel*?"

This time, she obeyed his command. Her hands moved as if of their own accord. She took the restraints from Paul's hand and held them nervously. Just the weight of them sent a ripple through her. They were heavy—twice as heavy, it felt, as the first pair. She ran her fingers over the softness of the black faux-fur padding; the touch of it on her fingertips made her *forearms* tingle.

Jasmine's mouth opened slightly and she inhaled at once through mouth and nose; it augmented the bouquet and she swooned again. In fact, she almost thought she was going to faint.

But by then, Paul had her by the hair, good and hard, gripped in his left hand, fingers laced through. He pulled, just a little, and Jasmine's mouth popped open wider, her mouth a silent O of need.

To cover her gasp, she whimpered, "I like them a lot."

Paul's hand slid out of her hair. Both arms went over her shoulders; he took the restraints from her hand.

One of the buckles was secured with a theft-prevention device, but the other was free. Paul unbuckled it, opened the restraint, and wrapped it around Jasmine's right wrist.

"Let's see if they fit," he said, closing the buckle quickly and skillfully. Jasmine undulated almost imperceptibly—*almost.*

The restraints were fitted with heavy D-rings on alternate sides from the buckles. Paul seized the ring in his right index finger and tugged, guiding Jasmine's wrist up. While his left hand came to rest, easily, on the curve of Jasmine's hip, Paul pulled her arm out to the side, forming her into half a *T,* or maybe something midway between a *T* and a *Y.*

She breathed deeply as he held her there. The leather smell was diminished, but other sensations rushed in quickly to fill the void in her senses. She felt the snug tautness of the furry restraints around her right wrist. She felt Paul holding her wrist up and very slightly back, restraining her with one finger. His fingers spread across her hip, his thumb caressing her back through the break between her top and her jeans.

"How does that feel?" he asked. "Is that right?"

"I think that's right," Jasmine moaned. She tried to say it brightly, casually, as if it was nothing more than an observation on the size. It came out as an embarrassingly sultry moan, but at least it wasn't as filthy as what she was thinking.

Paul's voice was softer, more controlled.

"Yes," he said. "It does seem just about right, doesn't it?"

Jasmine's eyes swam slightly. The rack of restraints became two racks, then four, then one again. Paul guided her wrist to her front again, and deftly unbuckled her.

Jasmine heard a perky voice behind them: the rainbow-haired store clerk.

"How are we doing over here?" the clerk asked. "You guys have any questions?"

Paul turned, and Jasmine could hear the smile in his voice, even as the air-conditioned breeze left an aching chill where his body had molded to hers.

"No question at all," grinned Paul. "We'll take 'em." The D-rings and buckles rattled as Paul handed them over.

TOUCH

Sophia Valenti

I n the dark, I think of nothing but his touch—of what his hands feel like on my naked, willing body.

I spend my days obsessed by aesthetics and the quest for visual beauty, as my passion is interior design. I think that's why Matt's so fond of blindfolding me. He says it puts me in my place, makes me more malleable. And when I'm bound and at his mercy, that's exactly how I feel: nearly molten and ready to be molded into whatever he desires.

All Matt has to do is cover my eyes, buckling the blindfold's straps snugly behind my head, and I instantly feel myself transform. And suddenly, the world is exactly as it should be.

My attention focuses on his gentle hands as they follow the curves of my body, priming me for any number of carnal delights. His fingertips stroke my breasts, the dip of my waist, the flare of my hips. My nerves tingle as if he's personally awakened each one with his methodical caresses. But I know his easy strokes are a temporary tease. Although I'm limp and supplicant, I'm well aware that when I fully relax, he'll shock my senses and send me reeling.

He takes his time, knowing that my anticipation increases exponentially with every second that passes. I'm writhing as much as I can, cuffed as I am to the padded sawhorse. Its rich leather fills my nose with its earthy perfume, and my heart is pounding in time to the lust pulsing deep in my cunt. My clit feels hot and desperate. I tilt my hips trying to create a little friction to ease my hunger, but it's not enough.

Matt pulls his hands away from my body, and I utter a low moan of disappointment that's quickly obliterated by a loud gasp when his hand connects with my ass. The heat from his palm spreads gradually outward from the point of impact. I hardly have time to catch my breath before his hand lands again and again. Pleasure-tinged pain suffuses my bound body, the darkness allowing me to absorb every nuance—from the sizzling slap of flesh against flesh to the glowing warmth that consumes my sex.

Matt's hand settles into a sexy rhythm, striking the left then the right, evenly heating both cheeks. I can't stifle my moans, and they only get louder as he continues. My entire ass is hot and tingling when Matt decides on a new target, focusing his wrath on my sweet spot. His palm, stiff and unyielding, strikes the center of my bottom, right above my pussy. The sensation reverberates through my sex. I rock rhythmically in time with each spank. By now, my slit is drenched and my clit is swollen enough that every motion of my body nudges it against the slippery leather beneath me. It's a featherlight caress that sparks a slow-burning desire and swells into a body-shaking climax.

Matt continues to spank me through my orgasm, telling how naughty I am for coming without permission. His words echo in my ears, making me come harder than I ever have. I'm still quivering and shaking when he's slipping his lube-drenched fingers into my ass, reminding me that a bad girl who misbehaves gets her ass fucked.

If that's the case, I don't ever want to be good.

Matt's holding my cheeks wide apart, and I feel my face flush hotly. It doesn't matter how many times he takes me this way, I'm still shy about it. Being bound like this lets me surrender to the pleasure, even when my nerves are rattled and I'm filled with embarrassment.

I struggle to catch my breath as he penetrates my back hole. The passing seconds are marked by the slow advance of his cock until he's balls deep. We exhale in unison, his fingers digging into my cheeks, as he holds on tightly and fucks my ass hard, aided by a river of lube.

My body relaxes, submitting to him fully, and as

TEMPTATION

Oleander Plume

Adam was below me holding the ladder, when a gust of wind tugged my skirt up over my hips, exposing everything. On the outside, I was dressed for fall weather: long flannel skirt, thick cardigan, kneesocks and hiking boots. Underneath, I was deliciously bare and turned on to the point of wetness.

"And I thought apple picking would be boring," Adam said with a chuckle.

I was on the second to last rung of the ladder, with my legs spread wide for leverage. Instead of pulling my skirt down, I arched my back to make the view a little more tantalizing.

"I'm going to need a taste of that." Adam picked an apple, then slid it back and forth over my dripping slit. I heard the snap of his teeth as he took a bite. "I can't decide which is juicier."

His tongue followed the trail the apple had taken, making me shiver. "What if someone—"

"Was watching? That would be pretty hot, but this place is deserted today." He rubbed the apple against my cunt again, then climbed the ladder until his body was pressed against mine. "Taste this, Eve."

He held the apple to my lips; I could smell my own arousal mingled with the scent of sweet fruit. I took a large bite, enjoying the decadent flavors that burst against my tongue. Adam pulled my arms up over my head and directed my hands to a higher branch. I gripped it tightly, but the ladder still swayed and my stomach dropped to my feet.

"We're going to fall."

"This ladder is rock solid." Adam picked another apple and waved it under my nose. "Let's see if you can hold this in your mouth until I make you come."

The precarious positioning mimicked being bound; the fruit served as an edible gag. Being caught in such a submissive stance made me tremble with desire. Adam unbuttoned my cardigan, exposing my bare breasts to the autumn chill. He pinched both nipples firmly enough to send a tiny shock of pleasurable pain rippling down my spine. I let out a small whine and he whispered in my ear. "Let's pretend someone is watching." He gathered up the front of my skirt and stroked his fingers over my cunt. "Shaved clean, just how I like it. I'll bet he likes it, too."

He teased my clit until I thought I would go mad, and my teeth bit deeper into the apple in an attempt to stifle myself. He pushed against my shoulders, forcing me to lean over. The branch I was holding shook, sending more apples raining down, and they bounced across the ground like red rubber balls. Adam patted my ass before sliding two fingers inside my aching cunt.

"So wet, I think you're ready for me to show our friend how much you love to ride my cock."

He unzipped, then got into position, causing the ladder to lurch, but the longing for a proper fuck chased away the fear of falling. His thick cock pushed against my opening, then drove deep. Imagining that there was an audience made the experience even more thrilling.

"He's stroking off while he watches." He reached in front and rubbed my clit. "I'll bet he wishes he were me right now."

I could almost feel the stranger's eyes roving over my body, and I felt my orgasm build to the point of no return.

"He's biting his bottom lip, I think he's about to go off. Uh, shit, so am I."

I came, even before Adam's words finished tickling my ear. My body dissolved into heavenly release then went limp. I watched the apple fall to the ground, bitten side up. Adam grunted before filling me with hot stickiness. I felt mellow and relaxed until I heard an unfamiliar groan.

"Adam, I thought you were kidding," I hissed.

"Sorry, Eve, it's not like I could have stopped the guy," Adam whispered back.

I heard rustling and then a man came into my line of vision. He was ruggedly handsome, clad in tight jeans that were open at the fly, his spent cock jiggled when he bent over to pick up my mock gag.

"Sorry to intrude, but you two are awful tempting." He grinned, then brought the fruit to his lips and took a bite.

It might have been a trick of the light, but I swear the snake tattoo on the back of his hand winked.

PRIDE IN MY WORK

Sommer Marsden

I made the mistake of making fun of Nadine's new apron. That's how I found myself tied up on the kitchen floor with said apron. A hot-pink and red number covered in tiny cherries. PAM'S PIE PALACE was emblazoned across the front. But I couldn't see that presently because the strings were binding my hands behind my back.

"You know how hard my week has been, starting this new job. I take pride in my work," she sighed, wedging her black heel against my ass. It hurt. And fuck it felt good. My cock was pressed against the linoleum and if she kept hurting me that way I thought it might punch through the floor and pop out the basement ceiling.

That made me laugh.

"You think this is funny?" she roared, digging the toe of her heel against my flank harder.

I sobbed, but my cock twitched too. I'm a pervert, you don't have to tell me.

She stood, leaving me there on my belly. Legs splayed, wrists bound, body aching from the odd position. I watched her spectacular legs as she walked to the fridge and reached up to rummage through the jars full of cooking tools. She walked back and though I couldn't get my head to tilt back that far, I heard her smacking her hand with something. If it was what I thought it was, my dick was definitely going to punch through the floor.

"What do you think is fair, Zachary?"

"I...I don't—" That's as far as I got before the almost delicate metal fish spatula smacked my ass hard enough to make me jump.

"I think I'll just go until I feel you've paid for being so mean to me."

"I didn't mean to be mean, baby," I groaned.

"You're a bad boy," she snarled. But even her snarls were cute.

Bad boy set me off, and as yet another stinging blow rained down, I found myself damn near humping the floor.

"Well, this day has taken an unusual turn," I gasped.

She froze. "You *still* think it's funny?" She sounded like she might cry. But that became irrelevant when the wire tool took another bite out of my right asscheek.

"I don't! I wasn't—I mean, god! I was just saying—"

"Not funny, not funny, not funny," she chanted as she whipped me with that infernal tool. My ass was a blaze of fire, my wrists screamed from how tightly she'd tied the apron strings, but my god, I'd have given anything to fuck her just then.

I froze when the fish flipper hit the deck near my head.

"I shouldn't even do this. You like it. That's no punishment."

True.

She grabbed a handful of my hair and my heart jackrabbited in my chest. "Up on your knees," Nadine said.

She'd dropped her retro pink waitress uniform and pushed down her purple panties. "Eat me," she said.

I moved toward her on my knees. A dull thudding pain had taken up in my shoulders and my neck but I didn't care. I leaned forward and dove in. Pushing my tongue into her wet folds, finding her warm sweetness and licking her until she pulled my hair and made me wince.

I wasn't sure if she thought this was punishment, but I loved this almost as much as being bound and whipped with cooking implements. I decided not to tell her.

I found her hard little clitoris with the tip of my tongue and flicked it and sucked it and circled it until her breath was short and she was moaning for me. "I forgive you," she gasped as she came. "Almost…"

I couldn't help but smile. There on my knees, my face wet with her juices, looking, I'm quite sure, like a moron. A very happy moron.

Nadine patted my head and said, "Good Zachary. I feel a little better."

Her black heels carried her behind me, and she untied me slowly. Then she was standing in front of me again pointing to her shoes. "Finish," she said. "Then you can clean up."

It only took a minute. A few jacks of my cock and I was coming. All over her pretty black shoes. I cleaned them up like her good boy. I too take pride in my work.

HOBBLE ME

Kristina Lloyd

I never thought I'd be someone who dresses for him, but now I'm a convert to lipsticks, heels and glamour. I totter in the shoes, feeling coltish and vulnerable, my toes pinching with the pain. I'm reminded of the times he made me crawl on the floor because at the end of each day, my feet bruised and swollen, that's what I want to do most.

I wear pencil skirts, hobble skirts, wiggle dresses and worse, and the underwear beneath them is severe. The scaffolding isn't pretty: flesh-colored shapewear to squeeze and suppress. I am hugged around my waist, hips and ass, just as I was when he mummified my body in clear, plastic wrap. I feel hugged but it's a cruel hug, stilling rather than comforting me. In the shapewear, I hold myself upright as I did when he made me stand naked with my arms outstretched, a shot glass of whisky in each palm. He thrashed me with the flogger, threatening worse punishments if I spilled any liquor. Inevitably, I spilled.

The clothes, as the names suggest, hobble me. I wiggle against their limits. Back then, my ankles were cuffed more times than I can recall. Once, he ordered me to fetch him a beer while I was shackled in leather and chains. I had to cross the room by taking tiny, Geishagirl steps, and he told me I was too slow to be his slave.

I wear lipsticks with names such as Burning Rose and Diva Red. My mouth looks full and flushed, a reminder of its appearance after he'd fucked me there with hard, careless strokes.

My fingernails are long and polished, preventing me from touching myself. I was never allowed to touch myself without his say-so. Sometimes, he wouldn't touch me either, or he'd touch only to torment, denying me my orgasm when I was begging for release.

It's been five weeks since he left town. My jeans and flats are languishing in my wardrobe. He promised me he'd return but he couldn't say when. In the meantime, I walk the streets dressed in my memories, wearing all my wants.

I sometimes wonder if he'll recognize me. He never asked for this sartorial performance. But I need to feel as if I'm always ready, fragile and awkward, a hungry gazelle waiting to be brought down by her lion.

JAKE HOLDS ME DOWN

Teresa Noelle Roberts

Jake holds me down as Remy fucks me from behind. My ass is in the air, but my head is down, pressed into the mattress, and my arms are stretched in front of me so Jake can hold my wrists. Remy strokes long and slow, in no hurry for his own orgasm or mine, and his hard grip on my hips adds to the excruciating pleasure.

I'm always restrained somehow when the two of them play with me. The bondage was Remy's fetish to begin with, but at this point, I can't imagine being with them without ropes or hands keeping me where they want me.

Jake's hands on my wrists are strong as any cuffs other lovers have used to keep me in my place and far sexier. Once in a while Jake bends and bites my shoulder, or tucks both of my small wrists into one big hand so he can caress or slap my dangling breasts. His touch inflames me further, especially since I know that when Remy is done with me, Jake will take his turn.

Mostly, though, Jake watches.

Sometimes when it's Jake's turn to fuck me, Remy will use his body to immobilize me, add to my torment and my pleasure. Holding my wrists as Jake does now. Cradling my upper body against his so I'm both trapped and embraced, imprisoned and loved, while Jake takes me. Often, though, he'll tie me to the bed with rope, or even old ties if we're too impatient to get out the rope, so he's free to do whatever he desires.

And what Remy desires varies greatly. Sometime it's fucking my face, his cock pounding into my mouth in a rhythm that matches Jake's in my cunt. Sometimes it's spanking me while I ride Jake, or slapping my breasts until my head reels from the fusion of pleasure and pain. And sometimes it's holding me as any lover might—except that someone else fucks me while he does—holding me and gently caressing me and kissing me senseless as Jake's hard cock drives me toward the brink.

But when it's Remy's turn to fuck me, Jake is always as he is now, holding me down and watching.

Watching my face and Remy's, the tableau of bodies, the play of Remy's skin, the rich amber-brown color of the cognac for which—no kidding—he is named, against my pale, freckled complexion. Watching Remy's dark cock as it moves in and out of my cunt, Remy's ass clenching as he drives into me.

Jake never moves his hands from my body. I think

that's so he remembers not to touch Remy, not to stroke that velvety cognac skin, not to kiss Remy's full, sensual mouth and most of all not to reach for Remy's cock. Jake desires me, needs me, uses me hard and unrelentingly when it's his turn.

But his eyes say he's in love with Remy.

And I'm pretty sure he's in love with Remy, like I am, for his dominance that doesn't need rope and whips and toys to express itself.

Jake gets off on topping me, fucking me, but I think he longs to lie under Remy like I do, while someone or something holds him down to be taken. To be helpless in the face of Remy's lust. I can see the need burning in Jake's eyes as he watches Remy. Feel the need in the strength of his grip on my wrists, as if I am a lifeline that will save him from himself.

I'd hold him down for Remy, pin him to the bed with my slight weight so Remy could plow his ass the way Jake craves. And I'd gaze at the sight of the two men I love together and get off on the beauty of their bodies colliding.

But Remy doesn't like men that way. He just likes sharing his sub with his best friend, gets off on our shared pleasure and seeing how Jake manhandles me. Maybe he's lying to himself and there's hope for Jake after all. But when the three of us are together, Remy can't take his eyes off me.

And Jake can't take his eyes off Remy, even when Jake's inside me and Remy holds me down.

MISADVENTURES ON A VELCRO WALL

Kathleen Tudor

She'd known it was a bad idea from the start, but the temptation was too great. Kris had slipped into the goofy jumpsuit, tiptoed out into the backyard and taken a running start toward the trampoline. Her body had soared through the air, and she'd let it twist and flip until, *splat*, she'd landed smack against the Velcro wall, which had been set up for her sorority's house party in the morning.

Upside down. In the dark. Alone.

She struggled against the Velcro and was shocked at how sticky the damn thing was. No matter how she twisted and pulled, it held her tight against the wall, and blood was already pooling in her head. She could call for help...but then everyone would know what sort of juvenile silliness she'd been up to.

"One arm. That's all I need." She braced as much as she could in her helpless position and tried to twist one arm free. How could a stupid suit of Velcro have her completely and utterly trapped?

"Babe?"

Oh, balls. She'd forgotten inviting her boyfriend over for some post-setup fun.

"Hi, John," she said, trying to sound casual. "Could you give me a hand with this?"

He was struggling not to laugh, and Kris thought she might have blushed if all her blood wasn't already in her face, anyway.

"How did you get up there?"

"I jumped, obviously."

"Clearly. Why?"

"Well I—we couldn't just set it up and not test it, right?"

"Clearly not." A snort escaped, followed by a snicker, and Kris jerked, wishing she had one damn hand free so she could smack him. Of course, if she had a hand free, she wouldn't *need* to smack him.

"Look, will you please just get me down?"

His laughter stopped all of a sudden, replaced with a wild grin and a light in his eyes. He paused to study her, and Kris resisted the urge to snap at him to hurry up. But when he finally moved, it wasn't toward her. John reached for the crotch of his pants, slowly stroking the bulge that had appeared there.

A bulge, Kris did not fail to notice, that was right

about eye-level for her at the moment.

"What will you give me for it?"

"John..."

"You have to pay toll, honey."

"Someone will hear us!"

"Everyone's either asleep or...busy. Come on, now..." He unzipped, and the sound sent a marvelous shudder down—or up—Kris's spine to lodge firmly between her legs. "Open wide..."

He stepped forward, his erection unsheathed before him, and Kris surprised herself by opening her mouth for him without hesitation, taking him in, strange angle and all. Strange, the difference that change in angle made. Like everything was brand new. She twisted her tongue around his cock, exploring and suckling as if for the first time.

John let out a low groan and braced himself against the stupid wall, his hips pumping slowly in and out of her mouth. Kris was dizzy from the blood in her head, dizzy from her mad flight, dizzy from arousal. If she had her hand free now, she'd unzip this ridiculous jumpsuit and let her fingers dance over her sex. Getting down could wait!

But she couldn't, so she focused on the only thing she could do. Her tongue fluttered, teased and stroked across his cock as John fucked her mouth, first slowly, and then with a quick, ragged intensity as she found sensitive places she'd never searched for before. She was so aroused she thought she might burst, and her hips made mini–pulsing motions, her muscles tightening, clenching, straining.

She began to whimper around John's cock, her entire awareness focused on the twin points of pleasure: his dick in her mouth and her clit, greedily sucking in every sensation it could. She sucked and teased with increasing desperation, as if she could transfer the sensation to herself if only she performed well enough…

And even without fingers or tongue on her sensitive bud, her body answered the fervent prayer her body was making, and she shuddered as pleasure washed through her in waves made unfamiliar by her upside-down orientation.

John's voice, harsh and distant: "Are you—? Oh, *fuck*, baby… Oh, holy fuck…" His salty heat hit the back of her throat and she swallowed instinctively, sucking until his cock stopped pulsing in her mouth, and he finally pulled away.

"That was—" He shook his head, his expression dazed, but Kris could only smile.

"The first installment. Now get me down and let's get inside so I can pay in full."

MINUTE TO MINUTE

Tenille Brown

She read somewhere that if you could make it a day, you could make it a week. If you could make it a week, you could make it a month. And if you could make it a month you could make it a year.

But this was the first day, and it had only been thirteen hours, and Jeanette wanted a cigarette bad.

Joe came in from work and caught her in the corner, sweating and bouncing her knee.

"You okay?"

"No, I'm not okay. I feel like I'm about to jump out of my skin, like I need to be tied down or something."

Jeanette realized as soon as she said it that Joe's mind would go there, that his eyes would dart across the room looking for something to bind her with. Most times she didn't even have to ask, but the fact that she had even made the suggestion in jest set Joe's dirty-minded wheels in motion.

"I didn't mean that literally, Joe," Jeanette said, but she hoped he didn't think she was protesting.

Joe held up a finger. "I know, but I think you might be onto something. This quitting smoking thing is hard. And maybe you aren't the type who can take it day by day. Maybe you're the type who has to take it hour by hour or even minute by minute."

By this time, he had made his way back to her with both sets of curtain ties in his hand, four ties in all, wrapping them around his wide palm.

The shaking had slowed, and the sweating had cooled. She was now focusing on the ties instead.

"The chair won't do," Joe said. "I'll need you on the bed."

Jeanette nodded and followed him to their master suite.

She knew that he needed her on the bed because the bed had high posts (the reason they bought the bed in the first place), perfect for attaching one's extremities to, and Jeanette was just the right length to lie flat on her back and stretch her arms and legs toward the four corners to be tightly bound.

"Get naked."

It was a soft command, but a command nonetheless and Jeanette quickly got rid of her tank top and shorts. She tossed her bra and panties on the floor near the nightstand, then crawled on top of the high queen-sized bed.

Joe unraveled the ties so that they hung from his hands. It was the first time in those thirteen hours that a cigarette was the farthest thing from her mind. What she was thinking of instead was being tightly bound, being barely able to move while Joe had his way.

Jeanette closed her eyes as Joe wound the toffee-colored strap around one wrist, tying it to the bed. He did the same with the other and followed suit with her ankles.

"Do you still want a smoke?"

"Not as much," Jeanette said, "but the urge is still there."

"Would you rather something else to get you through the day, through the hours, the minutes even?"

"Yes."

Joe had already joined her on the bed before she answered, hovering over her as he nestled between her legs. His beard and moustache grazed her thighs as he nuzzled her there leaving her to wonder...

Was he only going to touch?

Did he want to fuck?

Was he going to forget about it all and just tease her instead?

No...

Jeanette wiggled as she felt the moist heat from Joe's open mouth. He was going to use his tongue.

It was then that she became restless again, looking over at the clock as it changed from minute to minute. Jeanette was defenseless against Joe's tongue, even when her arms and legs were completely free. Even then she would scoot back on the bed, away from the torturous pleasure he would give her with his soft kisses on her pussy. She'd pull at his ears, clasp his head between her thighs so he would at least slow down.

He never did.

And here he was now, working his tongue slowly. Joe was mapping a wet trail along the folds of her slit, gently nipping at her swelling clit. Jeanette moved the only part of her that was free, lifting her middle off the mattress.

She met his mouth and he continued his tender assault rendering her helpless, and her body fell back onto the mattress. He was loud with his sucking and licking but it did little to distract from the feeling, the uncontrollable urge she had to come right then and there.

Still, the minutes went by. One or two he spent on her clit, three more nuzzling her thighs with his wet nose, another seven with his fingers in her pussy and then her rectum.

The minutes became too frustrating and Jeanette began counting in seconds instead, like how many it would take before she poured her climax into his mouth, onto his fingers and the bed.

It only took ten seconds more and she was vibrating from head to toe as if currents were running through her body. And Joe was smiling, licking his lips as he lifted himself from between her legs and began to untie her, one extremity at a time.

Lethargic now instead of restless, Jeanette made her way to the shower. She decided this was exactly how she would make it through the days, the weeks, the months with no cigarettes.

Lips to lips, second to second, minute to minute.

TOP GAME

Annabeth Leong

Nick grinned at Sandy when she strode into the party, domme boots clinking. "Lots of hot girls here tonight," he said, "begging for a sure hand and a rough rope. Need me to show you how to tie that Somerville Bowline you've been trying to get right for ten years now?"

Sandy narrowed her eyes at him, but smiled back. They liked to rib each other. "I'd have to find someone who knows a Somerville bowline from a granny knot," she answered, then whacked his sweet ass. His leather pants squeezed it into such a tight, firm shape that it smacked back, leaving her palm tingling.

"We should settle this once and for all." Nick leaned into her.

Sandy raised an eyebrow. Previous attempts to

"settle things" had resulted in one or the other of them more tied up than a female executive's schedule, being gloriously and mercilessly fucked. Sandy had always wished they would try to work out their differences more often.

She snaked her hand up the back of Nick's faux-torn shirt and yanked him close, sinking the tips of her nails into the base of his neck. "I'm going to give it to you so hard…" Lust drove the words through Sandy's clenched teeth with force and precision.

Nick danced away. "Ah-ah-ah. Who declared you top?"

"I'll fight you for it." Sandy reached for him, but he dodged.

"Remember those hot girls I mentioned?" Nick made a sweeping gesture that encompassed the surrounding sea of dimly lit flesh clad in latex, leather and PVC. "How about they decide?"

Sandy crossed her arms over her chest, plumping up her breasts even more than her corset already did. "What do you have in mind?"

Nick must have planned ahead, because with dizzying speed he lined up ten dazzling girls to act as judges. "First, we're going to do an aesthetic trial," he said, and Sandy found herself spinning a delicate dragonfly sleeve over the arms of a buxom, pale-haired beauty with biceps as chiseled as a Michelangelo.

She tied accent knots with glittering rope, then pulled

the woman close while she waited for Nick to finish his tie. "May I touch you?"

The blonde nodded vigorously, rubbing her hair against Sandy's nose. Sandy spread her fingers out over the woman's soft, round stomach and stroked her way up to the undersides of her breasts.

The group declared Nick winner for aesthetics, but Sandy didn't care because by then she'd bared the blonde's breasts and nibbled them until the other woman wriggled and hopped and shrieked. Admittedly, the pastime had ruined the neat lines of the sleeve.

The next test, "technical skill," wasn't nearly as fun because it only involved tying a double coin knot in the air while everyone watched. Sandy won, so that was something. She and Nick were tied.

Next, they tested speed. The judges divided into two groups of five, and Sandy went to work. She tied a chest harness on the first woman in line, lifting her breasts with careful loops and teasing her nipples into prisons of hemp. Keeping her rope continuous, Sandy attached the second woman to the first by the hair, so every shake of the second's head made the first's breasts jiggle. A simple double-column tie to the third woman's wrists trapped her fingers near the second's cunt—which, by the smell of things, had gotten very wet.

Across the way, Nick had chosen a faster but less creative method, tying hands together so that his submissives seemed engaged in a group hug, not a sex game.

Sandy didn't want him to win. She had plans. She

wanted to tie a nasty little web around his balls, attach it to his nipple rings, then lube his ass with the tip of one finger until his muscles fluttered beneath her touch and he begged for her strap-on.

She decided she didn't like letting Nick make the rules. She crossed to his side, pulling the three women she'd tied by the loose end of the rope. Nick's first submissive sighed when Sandy grabbed her and whipped a zigzagging lightning harness over her body. Sandy ran two thin ropes down between the woman's legs— the "happy knots" men tied never actually wound up rubbing the clit, so it worked better to run lines around the outer labia, squeezing moistening cunt lips together and drawing blood to the area.

Nick appeared moments later. "What are you doing?"

"Changing the game," Sandy said. She formed a quick, questioning loop around his wrist. "I want your ass."

"That's not fair," he said, but stood and pouted rather than moving away. He didn't look like a man who wanted to win.

Sandy grinned. She roped him with brutal efficiency, making sure he felt the crack and bite of the hemp against his skin. "Speed matters, but you can't be a lazy boy. You gave your girls boring ties. I think you'll have to make it up to them."

She pushed Nick to his knees, then tugged the subject of her most recent tie closer. The woman's inner labia, already a delicate purple, had deepened in color. The tips emerged from her trimmed, dark pubic hair, glistening. "Lick," Sandy ordered, and Nick dipped his head with adorable shyness and complied. Sandy nodded her approval and reached for the next judge so she could plan her next tie.

"You have a lot of pussies to please," she informed Nick as she considered. Her own pussy dripped, but she didn't like to rush. Sandy planned to wait until Nick could hardly work his jaw anymore, then ease the tip of her strap-on into his ass with exquisite patience, so slowly she'd make herself come three times before she even got all the way into him. She stroked the top of his head. She planned to settle things. She had all night.

IF ONLY

Kiki DeLovely

And I would begin to rock slowly on your lap. A playful game at first that nonetheless makes you hard and harder with every passing second, with each and every shifting of my weight to and fro, with the rhythmic motion that's profoundly imbedded in your muscle memory of more lascivious activities. The backs of my thighs pressing into the tops of yours, my ass sweetly stirring your cock. That delectable, hypnotic undulation would quickly morph into a more and more desperate writhing. Salacity and intent in my eyes while I grind against you. Wrapping my hands around the back of your neck, dragging my nails down slowly, as I'd lean into your ear and whisper, "Please, Sir?" The redolence of agony heavy and ragged on my breath, revealing just how badly I need you inside me right now…your mind still unconvinced as to whether or not I'm truly deserving of reward. Your hard-on not needing a moment's more persuasion.

Reaching up between us, you'd undo your belt as you hold my gaze steadily, sliding it off and onto the floor. A clatter of metal meeting hardwood floors. An ominous promise in your eyes. Discarded for now, later that leather would serve its purpose in driving home a lesson or two. Submissives ought to know better than to tease and taunt. The very sound of your zipper would cause me to drip all over its teeth as you release your cock, pulsing painfully yet still in control. The pristine willpower of control. You'd take your time in getting to that lesson, your dominance much more disciplined than I have ever been. That was before you'd decided to school me in the ways of suffering. A lifelong education. And after teasing my needy opening for much longer than either of us should be able to humanly withstand, rubbing the tip of your cock through my wetness over and over and over again, finally—at last—you'd command me to be still. Shaking with unfulfilled lust and abject longing, I would do my very best for you, following your orders, steeling myself, not moving an inch. The air fevered, the energy frenzied, but both of us would hold our gaze and breath resolutely. For an eternity or maybe more. Me unwilling to disobey, you'd be the first to exhale. Steady and unwavering, leading by example, giving me permission to follow in your wake. A gradual release of my lungs the only imperceptible shift in my otherwise motionless body. And gingerly, gently, with great care and precision, you'd stretch my lips apart even farther with one calloused hand—each movement measured and deliberate—while using the other to guide just the head of your cock inside me. My submissive stillness an act of altruism when everything in my being is begging for freedom, for more, for release, for more more more, for right now, damn it, for more than you'd ever dare dream, for the fury of yearning unleashed, for more, for untamed gratification, for more.

For more.

And I would be everything you'd command in that moment. If only you would let me.

THE GATE

Jade A. Waters

You clanked your glass against mine at the restaurant, then gazed around the area. I didn't think you were looking at anything in particular, but when you turned back to me, you smiled.

"After dinner, we're going there."

I followed the point of your finger to the shop down the row. It was closed—our restaurant was the last thing open, even with the late hours the locals kept—but its decadent iron gate was still open against the alleyway.

I swallowed my wine. It had been four days since we'd last made love, this vacation stealing every drop of energy and sending us to bed weary from all our walking. But when you gestured back at the gate, I understood why you'd brought your backpack to dinner. The flush that spread through me couldn't be from the wine—not after only two sips—and I wanted to rush to feel the surprise you had in store. Still, I knew the longer we took, the quieter the alley would be.

We took forever, too. No one seemed to mind the leisurely American couple, or the way we didn't speak, just stared at each other with half grins while you stroked my hand. When we finished, we wandered around the cobblestone center hand in hand. It wasn't until past one that you led me back to the gate.

"I haven't seen anyone for almost an hour. Are you ready, Mara?"

I nodded. My role now was to remain still, which is what I did as you removed the cuffs from your bag. I clenched my knees together, feeling a charge clamor up my thighs and straight into my pussy over the thought of being seen, and of what you would do to me once you bound me here.

You grinned under the streetlamps as you fastened me to either side of the gate, and once I was secure, your hands roamed around my neck and down my back. Then you kissed me and lifted my skirt, stroking my thighs right there in public. You gripped me, kneaded me, your breath hot on my cheek. You took my gasp as an invitation and slipped your fingertips under my panties, nudging them aside so you could feel how wet I was for you—and moaning when you discovered my short curls soaked through.

I wanted you to touch me deeper, but you liked to

string it out. You whispered, "How does it feel to be bound, my love?"

I pushed against your hand. "Good, so good."

You grabbed my hip, pressing your fingertips into the concave sweet spot that always made me want to cry. "Do you like to be under my control?"

"Yes," I whimpered. "James, yes."

You dug into your bag again and withdrew a blindfold from the front pouch. I smiled at your cleverness—I had missed you packing these toys when we left our apartment three weeks ago—but you covered my eyes so quickly I didn't speak. I knew you were testing how I'd react, blinded with the risk of others passing by and the wonder of what you'd do to me, spread like this. You nibbled my ear and dipped your fingers in me again, this time sinking them deep.

"Your pussy is the sweetest, warmest place," you said, and I clenched around you. I loved it when you told me these things, and I ground against your hand to show you so. In answer, you shoved yourself against my hip.

The want of not having you for days had taken over, as had the steady pressure of your fingers tunneling higher. I said, "Please." You elicit the strongest urges from me, so I begged. "Please, fill me."

You slid another finger inside. I wanted you to ravage me on the spot, and I tried to kiss you but you took your fingers away. You pulled back on my hips and arranged me until my ass was toward you despite the forward lean of my torso, then hitched my skirt high over my hips to expose my flesh to the air. Your hand connected with my cheeks—twice.

"Please, James!"

You removed my blindfold so I could turn back and see you loosen your pants. You didn't even undo them completely, slipping your cock out of the zipper slit and teasing me with the tip. I arched and pushed back against you until my face was numb with my tiny gasps for air, and only then did you slide so hard into me I cried out.

"Mara," you groaned. You were rough at first, but soon your hands were on me, around me, grazing my sides and caressing my breasts. You spread kisses over my skin as you pounded, then switched into softer strokes that made me never want it to end. It was a fast fuck to a gentle lovemaking, then back again, sending tingles over my skin. Beneath my panties, you raked your fingers against my swollen, aching clit, and the sounds I made weren't from me anymore; they were instinctual, carnal calls of need.

Suddenly, you thrust harder, faster. Your groans filled my ears, and your teeth scraped my neck. Despite the rough movement of your hands, I felt your tenderness—a calm just before you clutched me and plunged one more time. I came then, fluttering around you and moaning for the entire street to hear. Once I gasped, you panted against my back, your arms wrapped tightly around me as you trailed kisses over my skin. When you pulled away, you circled to face me. Your eyes shared such lust, such love, that I slumped, slightly, in my cuffs. You tucked yourself away and lowered my skirt before you unhooked me, and then you gathered me into your chest with a kiss.

"Shall we go back to our hotel for more?"

I nodded.

You took my hand and led me along the cobblestone, and we left the gate behind.

DON'T BREAK
THE CHAIN

Giselle Renarde

They're beautiful," Carrie said as she admired her bejeweled reflection. "Can I keep them?"

"Yes." He traced his fingers down her neck, over the diamonds and onyx set in platinum. "If..."

"If *what*?" Her breath escaped as he took her breasts in hand. She couldn't imagine where he'd found the ruby-studded pasties, but her nipples shimmered like ripe cherries in the sun. "What do you want me to do, Sir?"

"I'll show you."

His fingers tickled her sides as they rode the supple curve of her belly. She bit her lip to keep from laughing. He liked her to take these matters seriously.

Circling his wrists around hers, he fondled the vintage filigree of her silver bracelets. Her body was positively dripping with jewels. Her garnet earrings dropped like fresh blood to her shoulders, her fingers eaten alive by rings. This was absolute decadence. Luxury and nudity. Prestige and instinct.

"Tell me what you want," she pleaded. "I'll do anything."

Until now, he hadn't made any sudden movements. But darkness dawned in his eyes and he seemed larger than life, like a giant, or a mountain. Grasping her shoulders, he spun her until her belly met the back of his velvet chaise. Before she could catch her breath, he pushed her over the top. Her stomach cushioned the blow as her heels lifted off the ground. Her breasts swung low, but the ruby pasties didn't quite touch the chaise.

Her body formed a *V* suspended in midair as he held her wrists behind her back.

"I've decided to take the crop to your bottom." Dangling a fine string of gold before her eyes, he said, "But first, I'm going to clasp your wrists together with this chain. If the chain is intact when we finish, the jewels are yours to keep."

"Oh!" She smiled gleefully, kicking her feet in the air.

"But if you struggle too much and the chain breaks, you get nothing."

"Oh." Her body slumped so low that her breasts met velvet.

"In fact, you get less than nothing. I bought the dress you came in. It's mine and I'll keep it. The car you drove here? Mine, too."

Carrie's throat ran dry. She tried to swallow, but her mouth felt full of cotton.

"If you break the chain, my dear, you'll take the train home in nothing but your heels and jacket."

A whimper escaped her lips.

"Now hold very still."

"Yes, Sir."

The chain felt cool as water when it snaked across her skin. He wrapped it around one wrist, and then tighter around the other, avoiding the bracelets that had skimmed halfway down her arms. She moved with the chain, frightfully concerned. If she broke it, she'd be heading home naked. Well, naked under her Rag and Bone trench coat.

Public nudity had its own appeal, but onyx and rubies looked unfathomably fine against her porcelain skin. Jewels drew out the bloodthirsty winner in Carrie.

"Are you ready?" he asked.

She teetered over the back of the chaise. "Yes, Sir."

"I can't hear you," he said in an ominous singsong. Whisking the crop from the wall, he asked once more. "Are you ready, my pet?"

"Yes, Sir." The words strangled her, but the chain links tickled her wrists. Anticipation soaked her thighs. "More than ready."

She didn't have the strength to turn, but she could see him in her mind's eye. His shadow cast darkness across her backside as he let the crop flutter between her bum cheeks. She felt him everywhere, even though he wasn't technically touching her. The kiss of leather between her legs brought another whimper out from her lips.

Any second now, he would flick that crop back and bring it down unforgivingly. He would slice her flesh. Where? Which cheek? How hard?

Carrie shuddered against the velvet chaise. Her wrists rattled, bracelets clattered. Her breasts heaved against the cushion as she waited for it. When would it come? When would he punish her?

His darkness shifted, and she mistook motion for action. Before he'd even raised the crop, she flinched. A beginner's mistake. She jerked her head around and formed two fists, straining the muscles in her wrists, tugging in two directions.

Clicking his tongue against his teeth, he said, "Oh, dear…"

POP

Elise Hepner

$P_{op.}$

Sticky wetness pools between my breasts.

Another round, shimmery bubble floats toward my nose. I glow—iridescent from the harsh overhead lighting. His lips pull back in a rush of satisfaction, black hair slightly mussed. After months of play together he knows I'm his, but only here, at work in the toy aisle. Icy linoleum meets naked spine. Pressed back against the floor, teasing sensation will land, will soak—will find me.

He always finds me. We play our game of secrets, hiding our "relationship" from other coworkers, from ourselves too.

"Don't make a mess. Or you won't get a real touch."

Panties and jeans tangled around ankles. The tight press of doing forbidden things grounding us in the moment. His lingering, candy-cane breath flits between my thighs. I know he always wants me. Even his gaze across the store during work hours can't be ignored— even now while he glances upward from between my legs. Blue eyes smoldering with power and cockiness. Double-dutch rope bites my wrists raw where they're restrained above me.

Plasticky, acidic smells with shuddered breaths.

"Store opens soon." He purses his full lips to blow again.

Another liquid caress against my neck—a bare kiss.

Will they find us?

Pop.

UNBREAKABLE

Sophia Valenti

I couldn't remember how long I'd dreamed of this: of my body pressed tightly to hers, all softness and womanly curves. But in my fantasies we were alone, Cassandra and I. Reality was a much different story. We were standing in the center of the stage, our naked bodies nestled together, slightly off center. My boyfriend, Kevin, was wrapping bondage tape around our torsos, leaving our arms free but sealing us in an inescapable embrace. Glancing over Cassandra's shoulder, I saw her man, Russell. He was hefting a pair of wooden paddles in his hand as he eyed us hungrily.

I could tell she was nervous. Her skin was as slick as mine while we stood under the hot glare of the spotlight. Cassandra's rapid breaths kept time with my own, our breasts rising and falling, nipples peaking and whispering against one another's perfumed flesh. My high heels and her bare feet put us at the perfect height to scissor each other's thigh.

Cassandra fidgeted in place, her leg nudging my sex, and I released a soft moan in her ear. On hearing that noise, her knees seemed to buckle, and I felt the slick evidence of her arousal glide along my thigh. The moment was beautiful in its simplistic lust, but I knew this was only the beginning.

The hour was late, and there weren't many people left in the club. Though our audience was small, they weren't shy. I could make out their catcalls and murmurs of admiration over the pounding of my heart.

Cassandra and I found ourselves in this situation because we'd dared to steal away to the ladies' room together to make out in privacy—even though our lovers had told us that they'd decide when and where we'd have the chance to hook up. We were too impatient—too hot for a taste of each other's kisses. Our fingers were just starting to wander under each other's skirt when one of Kevin's dominatrix friends had dragged us outside and gleefully ratted us out. I wasn't surprised. Roxanne seemed to have a thing for watching me be punished. I could see her shadowy figure across the room, grateful for the bright lights that kept me from seeing the smug look that would no doubt be on her face.

But what I could see from my vantage point was Kevin walking over to Russell, who magnanimously handed him one of the paddles. My boyfriend tapped it against his palm, and I reflexively tensed my cheeks as he settled behind me.

"Relax—or it'll hurt even more," Kevin hissed in my ear, gently swatting my ass with the cool piece of wood. I wasn't sure if his words were advice or a warning, but I did my best to obey him.

Russell then approached us, shaking his head in mock disappointment.

"Running away to wank off in the bathroom like two little sluts," he murmured, yanking on Cassandra's hair. She gasped, and I could have sworn I felt her slit release a burst of honeyed wetness. "You both deliberately disobeyed our orders. What are we going to do with the two of you?"

"Spank them!" Roxanne shouted impatiently. I'd recognize her whiskey-soaked voice anywhere. I would have been angry if I wasn't so nervous.

"That's a good idea," answered Kevin, as if he hadn't thought of that already.

"Hug your girlfriend, Cassandra. Go on—don't be shy now."

Cassandra wrapped her arms around me, and reflexively, I did the same to her. The very next second, I heard the crack of the paddle against my flesh, my hips bucking forward as I felt heat sear my lower cheeks. I hugged her tightly, feeling her body tremble when Russell's paddle connected with her vulnerable ass.

The boys seemed to feed off of the energy of the crowd, their swats progressively landing harder and faster. Cassandra's delicate fingers clutched at my back as we writhed together. The heat in my face matched the increasing temperature of my bare ass. I was mortified that I was being punished in front of an audience, but even more so that they were going to watch me climax while it was happening. I tried to hold back, but Kevin's relentless spanking was making me wetter and more desperate, as was Cassandra's thigh as it wriggled against my swollen clit.

I was angry and annoyed and turned on beyond belief. I wished there was enough slack in our bonds that I could turn and lose myself in the distraction of Cassandra's kiss, but Kevin had been too clever. Bound as we were, we had no choice but to submit to their paddles and ride the waves of our undeniable lust.

Cassandra came first. I could tell by her helpless cries and frantic squirming. Her exultations of lust fired up Kevin, who landed that wicked paddle with fierce precision, smacking my sweet spot over and over again until I tossed my head back and cried out in surrender.

Kevin and Russell rushed to us then, seeing us on the verge of toppling. Their strong arms supported us and unfastened our bonds, but the one that now existed between Cassandra and me was unbreakable.

IN THE
MORNING

Jade A. Waters

"In the morning," Gabriel told me, "I expect you to show me how much you want me."

I didn't think much of the suggestion as my lover curled his body around me, then caressed my thighs until I fell asleep.

But in the morning, I awoke to a tugging on my wrists. We'd spent most of the night making love, so—groggy and weary—I opened my eyes to a slow, seductive smile spreading over his face as he leaned over and continued to manipulate my limbs.

"What are you doing?" I muttered.

"Binding you."

I was awake in seconds and wiggling my hands. Somehow, he'd shifted my arms behind my back without me ever stirring. Now he patted my wrists in satisfaction with the knots he'd pinned me in, and I felt an immediate rush of warmth between my thighs.

"I told you what I expected in the morning, darling."

Without another word, Gabriel crawled off the bed and stepped behind me. He'd bound me so many times before, and every time, I felt this way—this desperate longing, this hunger for his touch. The heat from my pussy seared up through me, and suddenly I wanted nothing more than to feel him, to lose myself in the way we moved together.

"Come to me," he said.

I squirmed beneath the covers, my arms pinned too closely to my back for me to use them in any useful fashion. I managed to roll to my side and slide off the bed, landing on my knees directly in front of him. Gabriel was naked, his beautiful prick swollen and upright before my face.

"Show me how much you want me, Katharine."

I grinned. Even bound like this, that would be an easy feat—I always wanted him, each second of every day. I wiggled closer, my balance off with my hands bound, and then I took him in my mouth. I swallowed him, licked him, wanting to devour every inch of him, and dear god, he tasted so delicious on my tongue, so tantalizing when I couldn't grab on to him or stroke his length. He jumped and jerked between my lips and I moaned, because I still wanted him so much more.

Gabriel groaned and I began to sway in my crouch, letting my heels rub against my cunt. I burned to have him inside of me, but I played along as best as I could.

His knees grew a little shaky, but without my hands, I couldn't really do any justice to the long drags of my lips toward the base of his cock. He pulled himself away and I whimpered, but Gabriel climbed on the bed, cupping my chin and turning my head so I could see him. He whispered, "Show me, Katharine." Then he lay back on the sheets, stretching gloriously out so I could marvel at the man that made me ache like I'd never felt before.

I yearned to do nothing more than show him how much I wanted him, but my possibilities were limited with the tied hands. I was so used to him dominating, smothering me in his caresses, and in this strange, submissive empowerment, I needed to get creative. I kissed him first, for his lips sent sparks through me every time my mouth met his. I did this for a long time, a passionate kiss to reiterate how much I wanted him. Then I climbed over him but faced away. Gabriel gasped at this maneuver, since he hadn't seen me at this angle in a while. I knew he'd like it—he had a perfect view of my hands bound and folded at my back, and of course of my ass, which he never ceased telling me he loved.

He said again, "Show me." Firm. Commanding. I was already dripping to feel him.

I had to concentrate as I lowered myself, for I had no hands to help, and Gabriel wasn't assisting in any way. But his shaft was rock hard, and I was so ready and wet. I eased myself over him with barely any fuss. As I sank down, I moaned at the feel of him impaling me.

He repeated, "Show me," but now his words were breathy. I arched and rocked, taking him all the way in, using my knees to help me grind and writhe against him. It seemed like only a minute until we were both moaning and crying out. His length was hitting me just right, and with me over him I had some control—and yet none with my hands bound. It was the perfect juxtaposition, sending my nerves into blissful spirals. And then he bucked in that ferocious, sexy way he always did before groaning, "Baby, love, show me!"

I ground hard, one last time, feeling him fill me so fast and deep I surrendered to it and followed with my own gasps. I lost myself right after him, all my lust for him tearing through me and shaking me to the core. For several minutes, we remained still—panting, recovering. I could hardly feel my legs as the time passed by.

Abruptly, Gabriel grabbed my wrists, tugging me down beside him. He kissed me and stared into my eyes. He didn't speak, only gazed at me in his loving way. Then he kissed me again.

He ran his hands along my arms and my cheeks. He said, "Now I understand. And I want you just as much, my sweet."

And then, all morning long, he showed me.

LOBSTER LOVER

Kristina Lloyd

S he sat in the restaurant at 8:00 o' clock, waiting.

He'd chosen the venue, not for its elegant cuisine or extensive wine list, but for the design and arrangement of its tables and chairs. The tables were draped in starched white linen, and the chairs were a classic, four-legged design; no fancy molding or banquettes. On her feet, as instructed, were the sandals she'd worn on the night they first met: blue raffia wedges with a ribbon tie that laced around the ankles like ballet shoes.

After ordering a Lillet Rouge, she bent down and used the ribbons to fasten each ankle to a chair leg, hoping the waiting staff wouldn't notice. She wore no underwear and had to sit with her legs spread wide, vulgar and graceless beneath the floral print dress and artfully tousled updo. When he arrived, handsome in a charcoal-gray suit, he put a hand on her shoulder and dryly said, "Please. Don't get up."

They chatted as if everything were normal; or at least, he did. She was ill at ease and a touch embarrassed, knowing she was only semi-functional. The restrictions made her feel at one remove from the world. She could not walk. She could not cross her legs. She couldn't discreetly scratch that itch on her shin with the heel of a shoe. She was pinned opposite him, her legs parted in an implicit display of accessibility.

Her discomfort intensified when the waiter took their order. Could he see her crass, open knees? Did he know her vulva was naked, wet and plump?

When the waiter left, her lover rose from his chair and came to lean over her, acting intimate by printing a kiss on her neck. He told her to raise a hand to table height, and when she did, he removed from his jacket pocket a roll of silver duct tape and a pair of nail scissors. Her face grew hot as he covered her hand with the tape, winding round and round from wrist to fingertips. People must have seen but nobody would stare or comment in a place like this where cutlery tinkled on china and violins played soothingly.

When he'd finished, her hand was a bandaged, silver stump, thick around the middle and tapering around her compressed fingers. She winced at the sight of it, hiding the blunt shape below the tablecloth while he repeated the action on her other hand. She hid the second stump similarly, her heart pounding as he returned to his seat.

Resting on her spread knees, each hand was a useless, clumsy monster.

He smiled, enjoying her disquiet. "We can pretend you're injured," he said, "and you're trialing pioneering new technology."

She desperately wished she didn't feel aroused by this, by him rendering her helpless and pretending he was healing her. It was so shameful. She remembered a night when over and over, he had hurt her. "Shh," he'd said, pausing to wipe away her tears. "It's for your own good."

He was such a kind sadist, the worst sort.

When the food arrived, she couldn't lift her cutlery to eat. The waiter made a fuss, worried the dishes weren't to her liking. She found it increasingly difficult to speak, her diminished agency subduing her into silence. All she could do was sit rigidly in her chair with her legs strapped apart, and the tape-wrapped stubs of her arms inert below the table. The hidden hands looked cyborgian to her, reminiscent of insulated pipes in unloved parts of buildings.

When their perplexed waiter removed her untouched plum soufflé and asked if they wanted coffee, she couldn't even shake her head. She felt more of a thing than a person. She'd become incapable of acting, instead becoming the recipient of other people's actions.

"Two espressos," he said, speaking for her.

When the bill was paid, he laced her sandals around her ankles so she could walk. She'd worn a thin, gold coat and he draped it over her shoulders, hiding her bulky silver hands as he ushered her out of the restaurant with old-fashioned gallantry.

Back at his place, he undressed himself before undressing her, then he drew them down together onto his soft, wide bed.

"Make love to me," he murmured.

And she tried, her hands like industrial lobster claws fused into single blobs. They roamed over his body, cumbersome and ugly, her weariness making them a weight to lift. Her arms soon tired. He smiled at her frustration. Destabilized, she kept on trying, shifting awkwardly on her fat, dumb stumps. She used her elbows to maneuver herself, rubbing her nakedness against his like an insistent cat. Her need for him became obsessive, desperate. She ached to touch him with her fingertips, to feel the texture of skin and hair, to trace hard and soft lines, and explore all his subtleties.

Because he had many subtleties, including the ability to dissect her desires and give form to strange longings she struggled to understand. She could never touch that skill. The injustice of it was cruel.

He surprised her that night by paddling his fingers inside her and rocking his thumb on her clit, taunting her with the dexterity she yearned for but lacked. He made her cry aloud as she came, her silver stumps thrashing on the mattress. This was her bliss, being steeped in a cruelty inseparable from kindness.

So she was happy for him to take over and consume her as he saw fit.

DIRTY
LAUNDRY

Brett Olsen

Another pair of Madeline's underwear hit me in the face.

I had just watched her take them off, so this was more than fine with me.

Gloriously naked, Madeline stood in the door of her laundry room and laughed.

"Here's another pair, *hamper!*"

The posture collar kept my head tipped slightly back, so the panties didn't fall off right away. They lingered on my face, dangling, creeping gradually lower on my nose. There wasn't much to them; they were little more than a slip of translucent pink material and a minimalist cotton crotch. I couldn't be sure, but they seemed to feel heavier on my nose than they ought to be; were they wet?

I took a deep breath. I could smell them more

strongly, now. These panties were very ripe...and yes, I was sure they were wet. They slid off of my nose and hung draped over the silver chain between my nipple clamps, as Madeline entered the laundry room. She retrieved her panties. She pressed them to her face, as if to check whether or not they were dirty—or dirty *enough*. She took a deep whiff.

"You don't even want to *know* what I did to get them so dirty." She smiled wickedly and tugged at my nipple chain, coaxing a yelp from my gagged-open mouth. "I wore them to the sex club," she said.

Had Madeline really worn these to "the sex club?" I didn't know. With Madeline, any adventure was possible. But it didn't make much difference if it was real or pretend; as she teased me, my hard cock gave a surge against the interior of the soft wet mountain that buried it.

Madeline balled up her panties and used two fingers to stuff them into my forced-open mouth. But was it really a mouth anymore? It would be more accurate to say that she stuffed the oral opening formed by the dental spreader that was an integral part of my head harness.

"But you like that, don't you, *hamper*? You like dirty panties? Well, I've been saving them up for you. I've got six more pair in my bedroom. You'll get every pair I've worn for the last two weeks. I bet you'll *really* like that, won't you?"

I nodded obediently, tasting the musk of her panties

on my tongue and smelling the roomful of dirty laundry that surrounded me.

Madeline laughed, turned, and wiggled her naked butt as she exited the laundry room. She paused in the door and bent over a little. My cock gave a surge against a deep wad of wet fabric. I trembled to see her naked pussy, its downy, dark fur trimmed to a patch. Her pussy was perfect…and oh so off limits.

But I could taste it, smell it…just as I could smell her whole body, around me—two weeks' worth of Madeline.

She left. Left alone, I worked my tongue tightly against the roof of my mouth, faintly tasting Madeline's sex.

I knelt on the floor of the laundry room. My wrists were secured to a bondage belt at my side. My knees were spread, my ankles in cuffs forced apart by a spreader bar. The head harness I wore had an integrated collar, made to keep my head erect semi-comfortably for a long period of time.

I was otherwise naked. Madeline's dirty laundry was piled up all around me, half-burying me. It almost reached the point on my belly at which the nipple-clamp chain hung.

Fourteen days of Madeline's discards piled around me, everything as aromatic as she could get it for me. She'd worked out each day, sometimes more than once, changing clothes each time just to get everything dirty for me that she possibly could. She'd even gone so far as to wear cotton T-shirts and tank tops, rather than the high-tech kind she usually favored. Cotton clothes didn't wick sweat away from her perfect body; retaining it, they become soiled with her musk.

Piled around me were skirts and socks and shorts and skinny jeans and sweatpants and five different swimsuits from Madeline's tanning-sessions out on her back deck—yellow bikini, black bikini, thong back, racerback, tankini. All of them smelled like suntan oil and female flesh; I knew because she'd rubbed them in my face before she'd let them join the pile.

I would wash all of them for her, yes. I would hand-wash the delicates and machine-wash the others. My hungry fingers would scrub out her lingerie, gloriously. I would love every minute.

But it wouldn't be allowed until I'd earned the privilege...by spending a little time as her hamper.

As voluminous and varied as the pile around me was, it was missing something. Per our agreement, Madeline had gone out of her way to keep her panties in a separate cache, next to her supposedly well-used bed. She'd been slipping each dirty pair on, coming in and rubbing them over my face.

She came back in, wearing nothing but her tight white athletic boyshorts and a baseball cap. The cap was baby-pink in color. Its front was emblazoned FILL-MORE FENCESITTERS—the bisexual softball team that Madeline sometimes played with.

My cock surged against her dirty, wet clothes, as I

watched her. In the doorway, she wriggled, sliding the boyshorts down over her hips, her thighs, past her knees, her ankles, her perfect bare feet with their red-painted toenails.

The boyshorts were visibly discolored a little around the crotch. She lifted them to her face, took a whiff.

"This pair has *sentimental value*," she said. "You'll really like them. Especially once I tell you what I did in the locker room this week..."

Madeline started toward me, laughing, holding up the filthy boyshorts and aiming for my face.

YES, MISTRESS

Erzabet Bishop

Sophie stared at the sapphire-blue corset displayed on the new-arrival wall and felt her insides clench. Taking the job at the upscale fetish shop had been a dream come true. For weeks she had been walking by the shop window, peering intently at the corsets inside. Her panties moistened every time she imagined how it would feel to pull the laces tight. What would the binding sensation feel like? It just wasn't enough to wonder. She had to know.

Trembling with hope and anticipation, she had applied for the job and now here she was. The interview had been especially harrowing. The shapely redhead who ran the store was model gorgeous and sported a different corset every day. Standing in the same room with her now, she wondered how she managed to get through the interview without soaking through her skirt.

"How are you liking the job so far?" Laura smiled at her from behind the counter, her hair pulled back in a tight bun that reminded Sophie of Mistresses she read about in her favorite BDSM novels. The tight black leather bustier and skirt barely covered her at all and Sophie felt her body clench in frustrated need.

Sophie swallowed hard and turned to her new boss, smiling. "I love it. Thanks again for hiring me."

Laura grinned. "Well, it was either that or put a bench outside the window."

Blushing, Sophie lowered her lashes and felt a blush creep up the back of her neck. It was true. Her panties were slick with want and she was going to have to do something about it soon.

"Get busy straightening. I need to go to the back to check in the new shipment. I'll be off the floor for a few minutes."

"Yes, Mistress." Sophie sucked in her breath. "Sorry. Too many bondage novels. I'll, um, get right on that."

Laura narrowed her eyes thoughtfully. "Okay then. I expect all the displays dusted and straightened when I get back." Sophie longingly watched as she made her way back to the storeroom. The short leather skirt left little to the imagination and Sophie had to stifle a moan at the image that crept into the back of her mind. She wanted to be on her knees, with her head between those gorgeous thighs. Sophie sighed and snapped back to reality. It was time to get to work.

Making her way around the shop, she straightened displays and fanned the clothing in the rounders. She tidied up the floggers and made sure the paddles were all in a row. She didn't much care for the latex items or the leather gear. Her eyes were on the corsets. Making sure each one on the wall was perfectly positioned, she found herself standing in front of the blue corset once again.

She reached out with trembling hands and took it off the hanger, letting her hands run all over the fine boning and lace. It was fan-fucking-tastic. Her slit was sopping wet and her mouth went dry. She had to have it. Mentally cursing her lack of a bank account, she gave a side-glance to see if her boss was watching and slipped into the changing room. Sliding off her top, panties and skirt she unclasped her bra and flung them onto the seat behind her. She had to try it on. Just once.

Undoing the hooks, Sophie slipped it over her breasts and pulled until the hooks closed. Well, mostly. It would take someone else to help her. She hadn't thought of that.

"Damn it," she whispered. She wanted to see what it would feel like until she could afford one of her own. The soft fabric and elegant boning felt so good against the softness of her skin.

"You know, that is a good way to get a spanking."

Sophie jumped, letting the corset fall to the ground, as she yelped. "Oh my god." Covering her chest with her arms, she felt tears biting at the back of her eyelids. "Please don't fire me."

Laura narrowed her eyes. "Well, that just depends, now doesn't it?" She pointed at the floor. "Pick it up."

Sophie bent down, shaking, and lovingly retrieved the shimmering blue corset from where it had landed. Her nipples hardened into tiny nubs of desire and gooseflesh sprung across her skin.

"I want you to bend over and put that ass out where I can see it." Laura vanished from the changing room momentarily and returned with a wooden paddle. "Do you know what this is?"

Looking back at her from the mirror, Sophie nodded. "Yes, Ma'am."

"Good. Now, I think I reserve the right to give you a good spanking, don't you?"

"You aren't going to call the police?" Sophie stammered.

Laura paused. "No. You didn't walk out the door now did you? But you have earned five swats. Take it like the slut I think you are and I may just reward you after all."

Sophie nodded, relieved, and braced herself. "Yes."

"Yes what?"

"Yes, Mistress."

"Excellent. I knew you had potential, brat or not." Laura raised her hand and let the paddle fly, connecting with Sophie's ass. The blows alternated from cheek to cheek, and Sophie winced and yelped as each one landed. She let out a sob when the last one connected with her sensitive and reddened flesh.

"Now, that's my girl." Laura rubbed the heat deeper in with every brush of her palm. "Such a lovely ass. Nice and pink." Laura laid the paddle down and let her hands roam along Sophie's curves. "Are you sorry?"

"Yes, Mistress."

"Good."

Laura stepped behind Sophie and ran her hand beneath her, tracing the edge of her mound with the tips of her fingers. "Do you think I should reward such a naughty slut for trying on corsets without me?"

"Oh yes, Mistress. Please." Sophie moaned as Laura slipped her fingers inside her sopping pussy.

"So do I, pet. So do I."

GETTING INTO TROUBLE

Laila Blake

A colorful rubber bouillabaisse is stewing in the kitchen sink. Pale yellow, red, blue, black, pink. The coagulating vapor smells sickly sweet of dish-soap and rubber. The water is still too hot to touch but I scrub at the dildos and plugs and beads anyway, relishing the sting. When my hands emerge, they are bright pink and a rainbow of rubber toys are drying on a piece of cloth.

I don't have permission to come. The simple one-word text message is still flickering in front of my inner eye as though burned into my retina. *No.* Just like the word was lit by the power of a hundred suns and now it is faintly superimposed on everything I see. Especially on his favorite dildo, the one that looks almost exactly like his cock. I try to turn away, try to sit and answer some emails, but before I know it, my phone is back in my hand.

Please? Please, Sir?

Drumming on the table, I start typing a URL, and after the first letter, my browser suggests porn. It knows us entirely too well. The front page is splattered with naked bodies in more positions than I can count, holes filled to the brim, faces overflowing in milky semen. Beautiful girls are suspended from the ceiling, their rope-burned legs forced open, faces slack with sweet exhaustion. My jaw tenses in jealousy; my phone stays silent.

I blend out faces and high heels and focus on the beautiful cocks deep in cunts and asses and mouths, on skin that strains in bondage, and can't stop staring, tingling, *wanting*.

Somewhere in the real world I have expenses to file and laundry to do but I can barely remember. *Please, please, please.* No message. The seconds tick by and my hand slips between my legs. I just want to feel how hot I am, how swollen, how needy, until I snap my hand away. I don't have permission to come. I try to repeat the phrase in my head and stare at the phone again.

I know I'm screwed when I click on a clip. Almost at random, as though my saving grace might lie in not exacerbating my indiscretion by taking pains to find exactly my kink, and yet I find a girl bound up like a parcel, strapped into utter stillness, more thing than being, slipping down on the evolutionary tree until she is more plant than animal: alive but motionless, defenseless. The moaning is enough, the smack of skin on skin, the low thuds, the fake cries.

I can touch myself , I think—there's no rule against that. I just can't come. The thought makes sense right now. I fetch the dildo and some lube—I can't come in my ass, right? But I can fuck myself, I can feel that sting of stretching flesh, driven by the subconscious knowledge that I am not supposed to do any of this and if it hurts, maybe that makes it okay. Except, the hurt is exactly what I want: as little lube as physically possible, no fingers first, just the dildo that is like Master's cock, mercilessly pressing against that ring of muscle until I can't take it anymore and rub my clit for help.

There are tears and saliva stains on my pillow when the cock sits deep in my ass, my muscles still contracting hard, fast and wonderfully painful against the intruder.

Somewhere from the hallway, I hear the click of a key turning in the lock.

I'm fucked.

BLINDINGLY OBVIOUS

Tamsin Flowers

There are times when we fail to see what might have been blindingly obvious to others for a heck of a long time. Here's an example: It never crossed my mind that I might like to top. Or that I might be pretty damn good it. That it might, in fact, be my thing. But once I'd tried it and got a taste for it, when I told my friend Mercy she just laughed and asked me why it had taken me so long to find out.

Why? I suppose because it was just something I didn't know anything about. In the three years I'd been dating Phil, we hadn't tried anything more BDSM than the odd occasion when Phil would tie my wrists to our slatted headboard so he could tongue-fuck me till I screamed the house down. And that's only the B part of BDSM, isn't it?

We went away to Paris for the weekend, and we were indulging in one of our favorite games: fantasy role-play. Phil had become my hot French lover, Pierre, and I had become his stern Teutonic mistress, Anna. So, of course, when we stumbled across an up-market sex toy boutique, we had to go inside and get some props.

At first, I felt a little awkward. I didn't know what to look at. But Phil's eyes lit up with pleasure—he became randy Pierre and his enthusiasm was infectious. I browsed the store, trying to imagine myself using the toys on offer, inventing scenarios for Pierre and Anna. Then I saw the blindfold, and I knew exactly what I wanted to do. I picked it up, a wide strip of plush black velvet, narrowing at the ends where it would be tied behind the head. It slipped and flowed through my fingers like liquid. I told Phil I wanted to surprise him and sent him out of the shop.

Back at the hotel, Phil was jittery with excitement.

"So what's the surprise, *ma petite?*"

His French accent made me laugh but then I became deadly serious. I took a step toward him and pushed him back until he had to sit down on the end of the bed. I glared down at him. I became Anna to his Pierre.

"It's time I told you something, Pierre," I said. "Your mistress is a dominatrix."

Pierre looked shocked and his Adam's apple bobbed up and down as he swallowed hard.

"You?" he said.

"Yes, me," I snapped. "And I'm not best pleased with your behavior so far this weekend."

"What do you mean?"

"I mean, I'm going to have to punish you."

Pierre's eyes widened and for just a second he went back to being Phil.

"I've never seen you like this," he said. There was a slight crack to his voice.

"That's because I'm Anna. Now, don't make your punishment any worse than it needs to be."

"Yes, Mistress."

He bowed his head and a shiver of excitement ran up through me. Good. The game was afoot.

"Strip," I said.

While he shrugged quickly out of his clothes, I took my bag from the sex shop into the bathroom and transformed myself into my new role. The black corset was a tad on the tight side but I loved the way it made my breasts spill out over the top. Stockings, stilettos and slash of red lipstick completed the look—I smiled at myself in the mirror. Then I picked up the blindfold.

Pierre was waiting for me, kneeling on the floor at the end of the bed. I wondered if he'd played this game before. If he had, it didn't stop him looking nervous. I paced the floor in front of him for a moment. I didn't want him to miss out on any of the details—the vertiginous height and sharpness of my heels, the stocking tops caressing the soft, pale flesh of my thighs, the tight curve of my waist or the eruption of décolletage at the top of the corset. Or the blindfold hanging loose in one of my hands. I was rewarded by his sharp intake of breath.

"Stand up," I said, going around behind him.

He obeyed, as I knew he would. His semierect cock bounced against his thigh, making my mouth water. I put one hand out to touch his shoulder and he flinched, only relaxing when I trailed my fingers down his back.

"Don't be nervous," I said. "I won't hurt you." Much.

Then I positioned the black velvet blindfold across his eyes and tied it securely at the back of his head.

"Anna?" he said.

"Did I give you permission to speak?"

He shook his head. He was always a fast learner.

"Now," I said. "Give me a safeword."

"But you said you wouldn't hurt me." He turned his head as he spoke, as if looking for me. But of course he could see nothing.

"Come on, play the game, Phil."

"You...you just sound a little serious about it."

"Safeword."

"Okay..."

"Okay? That's your safeword? That's not going to work."

"No. I just meant...okay. Bonaparte."

"Okay. Bonaparte."

I went back to the bathroom, where I'd left the bag from the shop. I decided to let him stew for a little. Build up the tension. Something inside me wanted this not to be a game. I wanted it to be for real. I wanted it to be Phil in that room, not Pierre, waiting for me with his heart pounding, a little bit scared and a lot excited by what I was about to do to him, even though he had no idea what that was.

I put my hand into the bag and withdrew my final purchase—a small, slim paddle, upholstered in matte-black leather. I had tested it on my hand in the shop and it had left a strip of red across my palm. The thought of replicating that on Phil's taut buttocks had made me wet then. Now, stroking the surface of the leather paddle and watching myself in the bathroom mirror was making my heart clamor. I took a deep breath and went back into the bedroom.

I wondered how it would be best to position Phil to give him maximum pain and maximum pleasure and quickly decided to take him over my lap. It was such an intimate thing I was about to do that I wanted us close together as it happened. I took his hand and led him silently over to the bed. We both sat down on the edge and then I bent him across my thighs. He realized what was happening—his breathing became short and tight—but he was completely pliant in my hands. His buttocks were like two golden orbs on my lap, the muscles hard and sculpted from miles of running along the seafront. I stroked them slowly. So beautiful, so sexy. And suddenly I was overwhelmed with the desire to mark them as mine.

"Pierre?" I said.

"Yes." His voice was barely a whisper.

"Your behavior these past two days has left a lot to be desired. Are you ready to take your punishment?"

"Yes, Mistress."

I picked up the paddle from where I'd laid it next to me on the bed. I took a deep breath, drew my arm back and administered the first blow. The sound of the leather on his flesh was something between a slap and a crack. The sound that issued from his mouth was between a grunt and a yelp. Together they were such sweet music, ringing in my ears as I watched the red strip intensify across his ass. His cock was pressed against my thigh and I felt it hardening in response to the blow. Heat flooded the area between my legs. God, I was wet and we'd only just begun.

"Count for me," I said.

"One."

I hit him again, this time across the other buttock. His moan was louder and his cock bucked against my leg.

"Two."

Again.

"Three."

My breath was coming in short, sharp gasps now. It was so sexy to hear him cry out and to feel his hips grinding against me with longing. My nipples were tingling and a sharp ache had blossomed inside me. I wanted him more than I'd ever wanted him in the three years we'd been together.

I only made it far as seven. The need became too much. I pushed him off my lap and onto the bed on his back. I pulled off the blindfold and he smiled at me. Then I climbed astride him and guided his cock inside. We both came almost instantaneously, as loud and as long as I can remember our ever coming together before.

And the luckiest thing about it? The day I discovered being a top was my thing was the same day that Phil discovered being a bottom was his. Fuck! How good does it get?

A SILKEN
THREAD

Kathleen Tudor

N ot now, honey, I'm knitting." Angelina brushed her husband away, and he stepped back with a huff of frustration.

"You're not knitting; you're winding a ball."

"I'm about to *start* knitting," she corrected, frowning at him.

Josh looked down at the couch and sighed. It was absolutely covered with yarn, except for the little spot where she perched to watch TV and knit, knit, knit. Gone were the days of snuggling in front of a movie or necking on the couch. When the fuck had *that* happened?

He picked up a ball of dove-gray cashmere and glared at it. "What's this?"

"A shawl, probably. Or maybe a scarf. Something lacy and beautiful and made to be worn right up near your face." She smiled dreamily and went back to winding the ball.

Josh wanted to shout. Instead, he picked up another skein, this one blue green with hints of dark black. "And this?"

"Socks," she said, not even looking up.

The third skein was marked as alpaca, and was fluffy and purple. He didn't even have to ask before she was looking to see what else he'd snared. "A hat for Judith. For her birthday."

"Her birthday was three months ago."

"I'll get to it," she said. Then she shrugged and went back to the yarn. The damn yarn. Always the fucking *yarn* lately! The next skein was interesting. Slippery, cool and a deep, dark plum, the label said it was silk and bamboo. It felt strong in his hand, like cord.

"I know what this is," he said. She looked at him, confused. "This one is a tie."

"A—?" She had hardly started to speak when he found the end and began to wrap it around her, quickly trapping her arms. "Josh, you'll tangle it!"

"So I'll untangle it, later." He wouldn't even mind. It was like water through his fingers, cool and smooth. And it went around her like a dream, binding her in shining dark ribbons.

"Okay, knock it off." She tried to tug one arm free, but he'd started high and moved low too quickly; she was caught from shoulder to waist. Her expression changed from mild irritation to something...more. "Josh?"

He paused in his wrap job to hook his fingers through several strands between her breasts and tug her to her feet. "If you don't want to take a break from the yarn to make love to your husband, that's fine. Let's work around that, shall we?"

His cock was growing at the thought, and he saw some answering spark of interest in her eyes as well. Shocking after all this time. He resumed wrapping, surprised at how long it took to get through the loops of silk in his hand. Some of the yarn went around her wrists in front of her, holding them together, and the rest went around and around and around until she shone with the purple strands.

By the time he tucked the end into the top of his wrap job, his cock was straining and her eyes were glazed and hungry for the first time in far too long. "Let's get you to the bedroom," he said, "you're all wrapped up like a birthday present, and I want to open you up."

And he did, pulling her pants away and tossing her panties aside before he tipped her gently back onto the bed and dove in to feast between her legs. Angelina moaned his name and strained against the soft, smooth yarn as he let the salty sweetness of her pussy flow over his tongue. He teased at her pearl and plunged his fingers into her depths until she was clenching around him and crying out.

Fuck, he'd missed that sound.

Only then, when she was ripe and ready, did he stand and position his cock. "Do you want me?"

"Yes!"

"More than you wish you were knitting right now?"

She let out a startled laugh. "Fuck you, Josh!"

"No, fuck *you*," he said, and with a grin, he did just that, angling his thrust to slide against her G-spot as he teased his thumb over her clit. She cried out, all teasing apparently forgotten, and Josh thrust again, plundering her body and giving back in the form of tiny caresses, each designed to drive her steadily back to the edge.

She got there before he did, screaming his name, her body tensing until he could see where the yarn dug into her skin. And then the clenching of her inner muscles proved too much for him, and he let himself fall along with her, calling her name as he gasped out his release.

It was several minutes before they were able stand, Angelina spinning slowly, laughing as Josh wound her silken bindings back into a harmless ball.

"So what's this one going to be, then?" he asked.

Angelina paused to kiss him. "You know, maybe I'll just leave that one as is." He smiled as she turned another slow pirouette. "Would you mind helping me clean off the couch?"

BEST FOOT FORWARD

Emily Bingham

He gasps as I plant my foot on the chair between his legs, which are opened enough to allow space for my foot to rest precariously close to his bare crotch. I smile sweetly to contrast the threat of my shoe edging closer to him, teasing until the gleaming leather is snug against his balls. He's so focused on holding my eye contact that he's oblivious to everything else. If he were paying attention he would catch a glimpse of the dark reinforced edge of my stockings as I raise my skirt.

My grin widens as I wait for him to notice that he's missing the show I'm putting on for him. The movement of my fingers meticulously pushing up the hem over my thigh eventually catches his eyes.

Snaking a finger under the elastic suspender of my garter belt, I watch him struggle: against his restraints, and to not speak. If his hands weren't forced behind him, bound to the chair, his fingers would already be clamoring to caress the softness of the stockings.

Knowing how much he enjoys removing pretty things from my legs, I make this last, emphasizing the fact that he can't participate. His instructions to stay silent mean he can't even beg me to change my mind.

Grasping the plastic nub of the garter clip at the front of my leg, I tweak it and sigh theatrically at the moment it comes lose from the loop. When I release my hold on the elastic, he's startled by the motion. Bending in nearly close enough that our faces touch, I reach behind my thigh to repeat the process on the other clip, his eyes widening as this garter also snaps. Without anything to hold it up, my nylon begins sliding down. I make a show of slowly rolling it farther, stopping periodically to assure he's properly engrossed.

Before I began, I told him not to make a peep or wiggle in his seat.

This intense slowness of my undressing and the placement of my foot are intended to emphasize my earlier instructions. I want him still and paying attention. He can, of course, choose to moan or angle his crotch closer to my leather-encased toes, but he and I both know the consequences he would face afterward. I have given him a suggestion that he's choosing to follow; watching my striptease or being reprimanded, he would enjoy both. I'm happy with his unspoken decision to allow me to continue.

I use his thigh for leverage as I push my foot out of the stiletto, letting the shoe then drop to the floor with a clatter. The spike of my heel has never seemed as weapon-like as when it comes to rest on his foot, causing a barely audible moan. I allow this complaint without consequence. I'm in a giving sort of mood.

I lift my toes from between his legs and pull the stocking from my foot.

"Open your mouth." His lips pop open and I gather the stocking into a ball, shoving it between his teeth. "Don't you dare drool on that; it's very expensive."

He looks concerned at his obvious inability to fulfill this request. This makes me laugh because in reality these cheap stockings were bought specifically for this purpose. I couldn't care less what happens to them.

Kicking off my remaining shoe, I bend down to remove my other stocking for use as a gag, wrapping it several times around his face then tying it tightly behind his head. His eyes plead with me as he makes all manner of noises trying to convince his body to not betray him. I have to admire his dedication.

He struggles with his gag and pulls against the ropes holding him to the chair. I'm pleased to see his cock— which had been timidly alert before—is now at full attention. It's a beautiful sight. I move to stand between his legs. To further mock his predicament, I spit on his cock. The feel of my warm fluid focuses his attention.

He looks up, waiting, slightly out of breath, his dick dancing with arousal and longing to be touched. I spit again on it, getting him good and wet before lifting my foot. This time, instead of placing my foot on the chair, I bring it gently to rest on his cock. Using my toes, I stroke and tickle the length of him. He can't seem to decide whether to keep his eyes on me or close them in bliss as I continue slowly rubbing my foot up and down. I relish the power of his dick under my foot, sloppy with my spit and his precome.

Just as he's arching himself into my teasing foot rub, I stop, wipe my toes off on his thigh and take a step back. I wait for him to gather his wits again before I remove my skirt to reveal the strap-on I've been hiding.

"I told you not to get my stockings wet," I say, while lubing up my fake phallus, rubbing its shaft.

ANYTHING BUT LOOSE

Tenille Brown

It didn't matter what happened next, whether she peeled off her leather slowly, exposing pieces of her cream skin in bits, or if she knelt before him, mouth open, worshipping his cock like he was king.

He was content with her right here, right now, pulling silk across his skin as she fastened one arm, one leg each to a bedpost, tickling his milky skin as she did so that his cock rose, stood and danced for her, and she for it.

She hovered, asked, "What next?"

And he said, "Anything, so long as you don't turn me loose."

D

Alison Tyler

It had never been so difficult to make a simple phone call. I picked up the receiver, put it down. Paced the office. Sat on the edge of the desk. Lay down on the leather sofa, my feet on the armrest.

I went out to the lounge. Got a coffee. Came back to the office. Pretended to work. Burnt my tongue on the too-hot java. Relished the pain.

What the fuck had I been doing answering personal ads anyway? I've got enough dates. Trust me, little girl, I get enough sex.

But I don't get the kind of sex I crave.

That's the problem. I knew that, and you knew that, too, once I'd written to you.

Why would I write to you? You needed someone who understood what he was doing. Who knew the ropes, so to speak. I wasn't a novice. I was less than a novice. I wasn't an anything. I only had the fantasies, the whisperings of something dark in my head all the time. Christ, all the fucking time.

You weren't the first ad I read. Not by years. But yours was the first I responded to. I liked everything about your words, and when you spelled out the scenario, I couldn't help myself. I came right there in my chair reading what you'd written. The movie theater. The bathroom. The handcuffs. The stall.

And now. Now I've had my hand on your ass, my cock in your cunt, and I want more. I want to take control. Not only of you, but of the situation. I want to be the one you look up to. I want you at my feet, leather collar around your throat, big eyes staring up at me. Waiting to hear what I have to say.

But I haven't done this before. I tell myself I don't know how to do this. I'm lying. I know. The commands are in my head. The desire is white hot, bone hard. I pick up the phone. This time, I don't put it down.

You answer and I hear the recognition in your tone when I say my name.

"That didn't take long," you say. "I thought it would be at least a week."

I look at the ticket stub on the forest-green blotter of my desk. I think how I could tear the paper into tiny pieces, sprinkle the confetti out on the sidewalk, go back to the make-believe world I've survived in for thirty-seven years.

Or I could say, "A tone like that will get your face

slapped."

You suck in your breath. You might have expected my call, but you weren't expecting this.

I say, "What are you wearing?"

It's like I can hear your lips curving upward. You say, "Black. I always wear black."

"Skirt or pants?"

"Skirt."

"Pull it up."

"Okay."

"That's not the way you respond," I tell you, stating the obvious. I cradle the phone against my shoulder, and I find that I'm running my left palm over my right, remembering the way it felt to spank you. The pain I caused. The heat there.

"Yes," you say. "I know." Because you're testing me. Little bitch, I'm going to win this game.

I breathe in deep, thinking about what I want. What I need. I say, "I'll be the one sending the instructions this time. If you want to continue, you'll see what you have to do."

"Yes," you say again, but this time, you add the missing word. "Yes, Sir," and I'm the one to smile now.

I hang up the phone, start the email to you. I name the hotel. I name the time. I tell you how to dress. All black you say? You'll wear white for me.

8:00 p.m., I type.

Every minute late is an extra stroke.

—D

PROPER PRESENTATION

Jacqueline Applebee

Kate wore my tie one evening; she was naked except for the strip of silk. She pressed me to a chair, her heavy breasts swaying as she moved. My erection strained in my tweed trousers as she unbuttoned my fly, knelt at my feet and opened her mouth wide. But before she could taste me, I slipped the tie from her neck, binding her wrists behind her back.

"You're tying me up with a tie?"

I nodded. "Now you may suck me."

Kate smiled up at me. "Thank you," she said, and then she swallowed me whole.

LEARNING
THE ROPES

Kathleen Tudor

Marley dug through the spangled pink gym bag and came up with a slender length of black leather. She grinned as she held it up in front of her. "Jenn, teach me to use this one!"

Jenn, her best friend since college, turned and cast a disapproving frown. "Absolutely not. We do *not* learn whips on a human target. Find the purple flogger." Then she turned her attention back to Jim. He'd looked professional and almost fatherly when he'd walked into the hotel room, his suit impeccable and his stature strong and powerful. He looked a lot different, now, stripped down and kneeling before Jenn.

The purple flogger had a thick, heavy handle, and the scent of leather wafted up as Marley freed its long tails from the bag. Each fall was as wide as her thumb, and she trailed her fingers through them eagerly as she brought it to where Jenn stood.

"Very good. I'm going to show you a little, and then Jim has agreed to let you practice on him. Isn't that right, darling?"

"Yes, Mistress," he answered. Jim was apparently one of Jenn's most loyal clients.

"Is he really paying for this?" Marley asked, surrendering the flogger.

"No, it's not really a full session. But I told him that I was teaching my sorority sister a trick or two for her birthday present, and he was very eager to volunteer to help, weren't you, darling?"

"Yes, Mistress," he said again. He straightened up on his knees and clasped his hands together behind his neck, and Marley felt a surge of eagerness and excitement. Jenn waved her back, and Marley took two careful steps away, her eyes fixed on the bare back that waited like a fresh canvas.

"The flogger is all about control and follow-through," Jenn began. "If you don't commit…" She swung it at him, but killed her momentum as she reached his back, and the tails fell like raindrops, making him tremble visibly. "It's all a tease. Watch how my arm moves, now." She swung again, this time adding a sharp, downward crack as the tails neared his back. Jim moaned softly, and his skin flushed red where she'd hit him. Marley bit her lip, trembling. "You control the sensation by how much of the tail you contact with. More tail means more thuddy.

Just the tips will sting like a bitch." She demonstrated. "Doesn't it, Jim?"

He gasped. "Yes, Mistress!"

"Your target area for now is going to be upper back and shoulders. Be careful not to get too close, or the falls will wrap." Jenn grinned. "You ready?"

"God, yes!" Marley had been ready since she'd done a bit of idle Googling and had found Jenn's pro-domme website and plenty of other *fascinating* fantasy material besides. Jenn had been surprisingly forthcoming about her unusual career, and had eventually even agreed to show her...the ropes.

When she took the flogger back, it was like reconnecting with a limb that she hadn't quite realized she'd lost. The weight was comforting and right in her hand, and she swished it through the air a couple of times, getting used to the feel of it in flight.

Her first throw was too hesitant, and the tails scattered across his back with no more force than rain or a light caress. Her second was sloppy, taking him across the shoulder blade instead of beside it, as she'd intended. But her third stroke landed perfectly, thudding hard against his back on the other side, leaving a gorgeous red mark that followed the line of his shoulder blade. Her entire body felt alive, focused on the skin in front of her as she painted it red like a blank canvas.

She experimented with distance, making some strikes slam into him like a fist and others score across his willing flesh like a cat's scratch, making him hiss in a breath and moan under her attentive care. His breath was shallow and fast, and so was hers, her pulse pounding and feverish beneath her skin.

Marley glanced at Jenn, who smiled knowingly. "He won't turn around until he's told," she said.

It wasn't much as hints go, but it was all Marley needed. She pulled the zipper of the plasticky catsuit, which she'd ordered online and hidden until today, and gasped at the sensation of cool air against her heated skin as the material parted. Still, she kept up the rhythm, steadily throwing the flogger, her aim getting better with every strike, Jim's back growing red with the criss-crossing of lash marks.

When the catsuit was undone to her waist, Marley shifted to reach awkwardly inside with her left hand, finding familiar, slick terrain slightly foreign with her off hand. She broke her rhythm for a moment, then her fingers found the hard little bead of her clit, and she let out a long breath and picked her rhythm back up, accompanying each crack of the flogger with an electrifying flick across her clit.

Soon both Marley and Jim were moaning softly in chorus as her body warmed under her own touch just as his was warming beneath the hard slap of the leather. She trembled, her whole body rising on the wave of pleasure, her arm keeping the perfect pace until she felt so completely undone that she couldn't control herself for another second. The pleasure washed over her as she let the flogger fall, and she let out one last, choked sound of erotic delight as she sank to her knees, trembling and replete.

Jenn was all efficiency, zipping Marley back up, taking the flogger, and attending to Jim, so Marley let herself bask in the glow of pleasure, both physical and deeper. Finally, she and her sorority sister—her mentor—were alone. Marley took a deep, shaky breath.

"What else can you teach me?"

TONGUE-TIED

Blacksilk

I could see Jess towering above my legs. She knelt in the middle of the mattress, while I, topsy-turvy, took up most of the top half. She ran her eyes over me, and her contraption, checking her work, ever diligent.

Her hands followed. First the cuffs at my wrists: not too tight, not too loose. The leather was the color of aubergines and felt buttery-soft on my skin. Her fingertips skated along a chain running from each cuff to each bedpost, then along the headboard until she reached the sturdy hooks she'd installed one afternoon while I sunbathed.

I wriggled, anxiously.

"Settle down," Jess said, eyes not diverting from their inspection.

Hemp, purple like the leatherwork, encircled both

the hooks and a spreader bar, which in turn held my ankles back over my head on each side. It was like she'd caught me napping mid-backward roll.

Her work surveyed and deemed worthy, Jess turned her attention to me. Fuck.

Her face was hard to read as her palm moved over my naked body. She cupped my ass with delight, a grin flashing like the single frame of a subliminal message. She leaned in closer.

She'd notice. Fuck.

"You took a shower before coming here, didn't you!"

I don't know how I thought she wouldn't notice, given her plans. I didn't know what to say, so I said nothing.

"You duplicitous bitch!" She said in a voice too light for real anger. Duplicitous. I shivered, loving a word well deployed.

"Don't you dare kink off that. I told you not to shower."

"Sorry, Jess." I mumbled.

There was a heavy pause.

"Sorry, Sir." I corrected.

"That's better." And for a moment I thought the matter was done with. Hell, I'm pretty sure I thought that right until the sting, because I damn sure didn't see her hand move.

"Ow, fuck!" The spank was vinegar sharp.

Ten more followed, quick like hammer blows. I

writhed and yelped, but neither got me very far. Jess's bondage was about as unrelenting as she was.

Ass in the air and heart in my mouth, I explained myself more readily than I might otherwise have done.

"I know you said you don't mind, but I mind, Jess. Sir." I felt ridiculous saying it, and speaking past my own pussy to her didn't help. "I just…you won't like it. I'll taste funny."

She got halfway through rolling her eyes before she stopped, looked me in the eye and placed her hand on my cunt, her rough thumb grazing my clitoris.

"I will. I promise." She said seriously, before turning mischievous in a way that made me wet. Wet? Wetter. "Besides, for once you're not in a position to do much about it."

She was right. Jess was a good lover, a great lover; she'd of course tried to give me head before. I'd agree, with reluctance, but pull back, knees together, often before she'd even touched lip to labia. I didn't mind. Sam had always said it smelt "weird" there, and Alex hadn't even wanted to try. So now I'd gotten older, neither did I.

Ever since our second date, I'd felt like I was disappointing Jess. And even like I might be missing out. Still, I couldn't get past that playground thought in my head: *Fishy fanny, fishy fanny!* Jess had tried everything but this.

Now I had nowhere to go.

She lowered her face toward my pussy. "You smell

too much like soap." She said. "That won't do at all."

Her thumb rolled around my clit as her other hand came down in firm, thudding spanks against my reddening bum and thighs. I yelped. I could feel how sodden I was, the sticky-slick glide of her skin over mine. God, no amount of soap was going to cover up what my pussy tasted like now.

Jess stuck the tip of her tongue out puckishly, eyes fixed on mine. She was just centimeters away when my nerves gave out. The muscles in my legs flexed involuntarily, trying to shrink back, draw in as always, like a time-lapse shot of a lily closing. But, lashed to the headboard with legs shoved apart, it was no use. I could wriggle, I like to wriggle, but nothing except our safeword could stop Jess tasting me now.

It'll be a cold day in hell before I'm using a safeword to avoid a little lick, I thought. Bottom I may be, but pussy I am not.

I scrunched up my face and felt her tongue-tip gently press against my vulva. I tensed against my bonds. I was so rigid, I could shatter.

But her beautiful rigging kept me a safe and secure hostage as her tongue began to work around the folds of my cunt. It wasn't just practical; I always felt better tied up. I sighed. It felt...good. Really good. What was she...? Oh!

Her hungry mouth had reached the little knot of fuck-me-now that was my clitoris and the sensation of her regular flicks and licks zipped through my body like a pulse. I clenched and unclenched my fists, I tugged at my cuffs and arched my back. It felt like nothing I'd ever felt before. I knew I was going to come. Jess's careful bondage was going to hold me down, and I was going to come while her tongue lapped up my most intimate of flavors.

Jess gripped my thighs and placed her lips around my clit, sucking firmly, sending me plunging into a climax that shattered the tension in my body like the surface of a frozen lake. I groaned, spasming, breathing hard, bucking, struggling…

She changed pace as my orgasm slowed, her head buried in my flesh, broad tongue sliding over my labia. Showing me—showing me she could handle the taste of my juices.

She resurfaced. "You taste like lemon icing."

I stared. "Is that… Do you even like lemon icing?"

"Fuck yes, I like it." She grinned and reburied her head.

FIRE AND STEEL

Christian Faraday

Mallory had run hot and cold from the moment I met her, but that all changed in one ecstatic evening. I'd been so proud of myself, thinking I'd finally made a breakthrough when she'd accepted my invitation for drinks. But before the night was through, I learned that my flattery and flirtatious banter had done little to sway her. Mallory never did anything—or anyone—until she was ready. A pair of sturdy metal cuffs and the menacing sight of a lit, tilted candle taught me that lesson—one I'll never forget.

Since Mallory moved into the apartment down the hall, she'd been alternately flirtatious and distant. Though her attitude didn't matter to my libido one bit. In the morning, the click-clack of her high-heeled boots in the hallway was like a siren's call. I'd grab my keys and hustle out the door, eager to share the two-minute elevator ride with her perfumed presence. She was a noirish goddess with flame-red hair styled in soft waves, glossy crimson lips and milky-white skin. I tried to sneak glances at her generous curves without seeming lecherous and always remembered to say good morning. If she was preoccupied, I might get a nod of acknowl-edgment. If she was in a more generous mood, I'd get a smile. Either scenario left me with a painfully erect cock and indecent fantasies that would last throughout my entire commute.

That night at the bar, Mallory only got halfway through her club soda with a twist of lime before she suggested we go back to her apartment. I'd only had a few sips of whiskey, but I already felt drunk from the lust welling within me.

We'd barely entered her apartment when Mallory took hold of my tie and led me straight to her dimly lit bedroom. I bit back a smile as she undressed me. I quickly got the impression that she was in charge. This was Mallory's world, and I was grateful to be a small part of it.

"On the bed, mister," she said playfully, once I was totally naked. My cock was already fully erect, but she accepted my state as the compliment it was.

I licked my lips and reached over my head, grabbing on to the rails of her headboard.

"Oh, that's exactly how I want you," she whispered, her eyes sparkling wickedly. I couldn't hide my surprise when she pulled a pair of shiny cuffs from her night-stand and fastened them around my wrists, but the click of each cuff sent a jolt to my cock. I'd never been bound before, but having those rings of metal encasing my wrists caused a change in me. I was no longer the pursuer; I was her plaything.

I gave a tug, which told me right away that Mallory had woven the cuffs' connecting chain through the headboard slats to pin my hands in place. The jangle of metal—the sound of my struggle—made her grin, and now Mallory seemed to be in more of a rush. She discarded her clothes hastily, revealing her stunning beauty to me for the first time. My eyes followed her every move as she lit a taper on her nightstand. She carefully extricated the candle from its holder and then sensuously straddled my pelvis.

Mallory settled her slit against me, pinning my throbbing cock to my stomach. I could feel her heat and wetness, which fed my increasing desperation. The reflection from the candlelight danced in her emerald eyes as she tilted the taper ever so slowly. Time seemed to still, and my breath definitely did, as she let a drop of molten wax drop onto my chest. The warm sting elic-ited a gasp from my lips and a jolt from my cock. Her expression grew more lustful and eager.

Raising her hips, Mallory reached down with her free hand to position my erection at her entrance. She kept her eyes locked on mine as she lowered herself onto my shaft. At the same time, she drizzled more of that devilish wax onto my chest, its sharp spark making my hips lurch upward. The snug embrace of her wet cunt was my reward for the pain I so willingly received—as much and as often as she wanted to deliver it.

Every moan, every gasp that I uttered fanned the flames of her desire. She rode me harder and faster, painting my flesh with slashes of liquid wax. Pleasure and pain became one, and I was forever lost in the communion of our flesh, consumed by fire and steel— and Mallory.

7:00 A.M.

G. C. Elizabeth

I admire your nakedness through sleepy lenses and a lover's haze, already missing your weight pressing me into the mattress as you bury your erection deep inside me, slowly stroking that gorgeous length of yours. I do my best to remember how you looked and felt on top of me, taking advantage of the fact that now my hands are free, and quietly slide my fingers between my legs.

I spread my sex with my left hand using my right index and middle fingers to start on my clit. I concentrate on the wideness of your stance in front of the mirror, the positioning of your body golden and triumphant, Herculean and godlike as you begin your morning routine.

"Do you have to go?" I plaintively inquire through the bleariness of an early morning whisper. You recognize the slight moan in my undertone and fix your eyes on the cloud of fluffy white linens I'm squirming underneath, the lightness of their texture feeling oh so good against my nakedness—new and luxurious like the hotel we're staying in.

I wriggle against my fingers doing my best to mimic the motion of yours through your short black hair, imagining that you're circling the stinging ball of my clit the same way you massage gel into your waves right now.

"What are you doing under there?" you say perceptively through a crooked grin, wiping your hands on a towel before making your way around to my side of the bed. I flush red, knowing that you usually like to do this yourself.

"The team will be picking me up from the lobby in twenty minutes and it would be highly unprofessional for me to greet them with a massive hard-on."

"Don't go," I whine. "They'll understand that you had to fuck me silly."

You chuckle at my dreadful attempt at a joke and kiss my forehead.

"I have to, baby," you say regretfully. Somehow the playful pout you give reminds me that you'll only be gone for a few hours, and that I should be patient. This *is* a business trip for you after all, not just a weekend of lovemaking at the company's expense. The signing of this contract could finally mean partner for you at the firm.

"Plus"—you catch me by surprise when you suddenly lift the section of comforter covering my hips, removing

my hands from my pussy to replace them with yours—
"I'm looking forward to getting back here and taking
full advantage of your undivided attention."

Mmm. I moan at many mischievous thoughts as
you easily slip two long fingers inside me with my slickness. Your fingers curl over and over inside me, telling
my orgasm to *come here* while you massage my clit with
your thumb. The sensation makes my hips wave and
I close my eyes, relaxing into the pillow to savor the
gentle fullness of your male touch.

"Oooh god, yeah…"

Impulsively I reach to take hold of your forearm
wanting desperately to pump into you, to take you deeper,
but you catch me with the quickness of your free hand,
clamping my wrists together with the strength of your
grasp—the accuracy of your sudden move reminding me
of your collegiate years playing baseball.

I wince and moan at the juxtaposition of desperately
wanting to touch you, but being unbelievably turned on
by the notion of my submission pleasing you.

You close tighter around my hands. I rock as your
thumb continues pressing and rolling my clit, the edge
of it tickling the soft ginger patch of hair above my slit,
delicately brushing against the wisps you like to play
with sometimes while we lie doing nothing in bed.

"That a girl," you reply as my breathing shallows,
becoming more rapid, "Come for me, baby."

The low rumble of your voice slithers into my core,
right where the pulsing begins…

I cry out clinching tightly to nothing, restricted by your grasp as I push my orgasm out, twitching and jerking against you, riding your hand and every convulsing wave to shore.

I'm filled with guilty pleasure when I finally notice your huge erection, taking hold of it when you release my hands.

You groan as I work the swell of your desire, my nipples tightening in instant arousal at how greedily you continue helping yourself to my pussy. You pump into my grip, helping me keep a steady rhythm, positioning your body directly over me a moment later. Instinctively I part my lips, moving up and down your shaft a few more beats before angling the tip of your dick toward my now fully open mouth. I focus intently on your hole just as it begins to heat, swell, then pulse....

You let out a deep burning sound as warm liquid spills from you. I lap around the glistening head of your cock, squeezing just below its ridge to drain you into my mouth. *"Jesus, god..."* you testify as I lick you clean, as I show you just how much I appreciate you, "What am I going to do with you?"

SAFETY
SHEARS

Jade A. Waters

Is it too tight?"

Julia tore her gaze from Matthew, which was a challenge, considering he could wet her panties just by staring at her with that look on his face. It was the same look he'd given her when he met her four months ago, before he put his hand on her knee and said, "I'd love to tie you up some day, beautiful."

She swallowed at the memory, then eyed the ropes binding her wrists. They scratched at her skin when she wiggled her hands. The nylon wasn't her favorite material, to be sure—her dominatrix friend had spent hours teaching her the different kinds of rope for this sort of thing, as well as numerous safe ties. What Matthew had done was a little questionable, but she still felt safe beneath his handiwork.

"I think it's okay," she said, clenching a hand, then releasing it. She smiled at him. "You have the safety shears handy, right?"

He nodded, jumping off the bed to show her that he did indeed have them, right there on the nightstand. When he stood upright, the glow from her lamp cast the sexiest of shadows over his abdomen, enhancing the results of all the working out he'd done of late. He was such a pleasure to look at, the most handsome lover Julia had taken in years. And with the eager way he stared at her, he'd proven delightful in more ways than one.

"Of course. I wouldn't want to give you carpal tunnel. Or anything worse. Can you imagine?" Matthew chuckled and crawled between her thighs again, but now he grew serious, quiet. He admired his work. "Dear god, you're beautiful like this."

Julia had only been cuffed before, but something about Matthew made her want to submit to his every whim. He'd spent the last twenty minutes binding her like a man possessed, stopping every so often to caress her face or brush back her hair. Twice he'd slipped a finger inside her, testing her and moaning at how her pussy flinched around him. "Please, Matthew, fuck me," she'd cried, and he'd hurried back to the business of tying her up. Now he ran his hands over her inner thighs and down to her ankles, fondling the rope that connected them to her wrists. Instead of the traditional hog or frog tie, he'd left her on her back with her legs splayed and her thighs free so he could more easily access her. And he did just that, tracing back from the ties and over her belly, then circling his fingers around her nipples and making her gasp.

"I need you," she whispered.

"And I you." The tender way he ran his fingers along her neck made her squirm. Matthew crawled over her, trailing his lips over the side of her face, then sliding his hand down to meet her sex. She had been drenched from the moment he'd stripped off her clothes, and yet, when he grazed his fingers over her opening, he moaned in surprise. "My love, you're incredible."

Julia shuddered as he pushed three fingers inside her—no warm-up, no tease. She didn't need it. And as he pressed up into her core, she gasped.

"May I fuck you like this, Julia? My beautiful Julia?"

She nodded, trembling. He could do anything to her with those eyes, with that touch. He lowered himself, and when he nudged her legs farther apart, the tension on her wrists sent her heart racing. Matthew guided himself in and Julia moaned, muttering, "Yes, yes, yes…"

He sank deep, his excitement creating the faintest beads of sweat along his hairline. He wrapped his hands around her thighs right at the base of her hips and squeezed like she loved, then thrust into her again.

"Oh Julia…" Matthew covered her mouth with his, giving her the deepest kiss as he pressed again. Her insides stormed, shook, all of her being threatening to explode in the most intense pleasure bound like this.

Matthew's tongue sought every surface in her mouth while he buried himself inside her, and his strokes grew faster and more frenzied. This was new for him too, and Julia could see it in his playful gaze and hungry smile.

"Yes, Matthew, god," she growled. With his hands all over her, his cock filling her and the rub of the rope on her skin, she was drowning in pleasure. She closed her eyes, her whimpers turning into desperate cries. Matthew drove harder, riding the bucks she tried to make while pinned beneath him.

"Oh…" He thrust one more time and Julia howled. Her walls shuddered and squeezed, pulling him deeper. "Oh shit, oh," Matthew said, and in an instant, he was coming with her, both of them groaning until he collapsed over her with a heavy cough.

For several minutes, Matthew lay with his cheek against her breast and his hand draped over the ties on her ankle. When he caught his breath, he smiled at her.

"You are stunning," he said.

"You too," Julia said. Her face was numb, and the aftershocks still ran through her pussy. She tested her limbs, noticing her left hand was slightly numb. "I might need to be untied on the left pretty soon here."

"Oh crap!" Matthew was up in a second, swooping the shears off the table and clipping her free. He wiped at his brow and Julia giggled at his immediate panic coupled with the fresh rush of blood to her wrist.

"It wasn't an emergency, silly," she said. "And now you ruined the rope!"

"Doesn't matter." Matthew caressed her wrist and arm. He cradled her limb in his lap, massaging her hand. "No pain for my beauty."

"Well, some." Julia winked.

"Yes." Matthew raised her hand to his mouth and kissed her fingertips. Then he grinned. "I brought more rope, you know."

POWER STRUGGLE

Angell Brooks

You take my power.

Take away my right to choose.

Slide the shackles up my arms, the smooth metal cold on my skin.

Tighten them in place with a controlled fury.

Notice the desire between my legs, the flush of my breasts, the want in my eyes.

Know I've misbehaved on purpose. Know that I conspired to incur your wrath.

Know that I know that you want me this way.

So take my power, take my rights. Make me helpless.

And then make me yours.

Tie me up—and then take me higher.

Until I come...down hard.

STRANGE ARRIVAL

Annabeth Leong

For a long time, Lynn could imagine nothing more thrilling than to sit at the feet of a man, naked, collared and waiting. She thought just five minutes of this would make her happy, even if he never touched her. She could not advance her fantasy beyond that moment, could not begin to think about what might happen next.

Lynn had these thoughts while married to a man she couldn't even breathe them to. She confessed them exactly once, to her glamorous friend Sheena, who responded by giving Lynn a long, cat-eyed stare, then pouring her another glass of wine.

After Lynn left her husband, Sheena surprised her early one morning, appearing at the door as breathless as if she had run the entire way to Lynn's little efficiency. She'd dressed for evening, her blonde hair piled on top of her head in harsh, architectural ringlets and her curves bracketed and lifted by shimmering, embellished cloth.

"Does it have to be a man?"

Lynn blinked, confused, and for explanation Sheena produced a slender collar from her purse, the animal scent of new leather rolling off it in waves. She laid it on Lynn's kitchen table, then took a seat and crossed her arms over her chest. Aside from her hyperventilation, Sheena presented a perfect picture of detachment.

The collar beckoned from the table, oiled and gleaming. Lynn approached, running one finger around the edge of it so lightly that she could barely feel it at all. It bore no design or decoration. It rested in a smooth, perfect circle, uninterrupted apart from its dull, simple buckle.

In her fantasies, Lynn's heart pounded at a moment like this, and she bit her lip shyly. Instead, one slow, decisive pulse traveled through her body, leaving fire in its wake. She couldn't have been shy after that if she'd wanted to.

Lynn lifted her chin to meet Sheena's gaze, and reached for the first button of the pajama top she still wore. A slight nod from Sheena, and Lynn had no more hesitations. She undid every button, letting her top fall open to reveal the roundness of her breasts and belly. She shrugged out of it and folded it, relieved that she never wore underwear to bed. She couldn't have withstood any more tension than she already felt, any more barriers between herself and what Sheena offered.

She stepped out of her pajama bottoms, embarrassed that her perfectly made-up friend would see that she didn't wax or shave her pubic hair. She did not let the worry stop her. Lynn set the pants aside and sank to the tile of her own kitchen floor, the hard surface uncomfortable against her knees.

The legs of Sheena's chair scraped the floor in a smooth arc that ended beside Lynn. Sheena's palm rested on Lynn's head, and her long, rounded fingernails delved into Lynn's hair until they lightly scratched her scalp.

Sheena's ragged panting echoed through the kitchen. The collar's metal buckle clicked and rang against the wooden surface of the table. Nothing had really even happened yet, and still Lynn struggled not to squirm, the growing wetness between her legs making her achy and restless. A sharp, salty scent announced Sheena's similar condition.

A finger of leather stroked across Lynn's bare shoulder. She shivered and gasped. A tongue to the clit could not have shot more arousal through her body.

"Is this okay?" Sheena whispered.

Lynn swallowed, her throat so tight with desire that she could hardly make her voice work. "Very."

Sheena laughed softly and curled the leather into a loose circle around Lynn's neck. Lynn closed her eyes. The incidental brushes of Sheena's fingers as she buckled the collar closed were almost more than she could bear.

Leather whispered against leather as Sheena drew the excess length through the fastening loop. She pulled

Lynn against her leg, the subtle embroidered pattern of her tights pressing into Lynn's cheek. The intimacy of the moment paralyzed Lynn, even as her body vibrated with intensified sensation.

She didn't know how long they sat that way, only that she could have done it forever, her mind blank with bliss. Blood crawled through Lynn's veins, breath clawed in and out of her lungs and her cunt pulsed as if her heart had moved there.

Eventually, light strokes on Lynn's neck eased her out of the reverie. Sheena removed the collar with the same elegant precision she'd used to put it on. She pulled Lynn up into her lap, and Lynn collapsed against her, inexplicably exhausted.

"I want to watch you touch yourself," Sheena said. When Lynn nodded, Sheena guided Lynn's hand down her belly.

Despite its familiar features, Lynn's pussy felt alien to her now. Beneath her fingertips, it swelled larger, hotter and wetter than she could ever recall it being. She burrowed against Sheena as she explored this transformed part of herself, surrounded by silk and perfume and softness. She drew back the hood from her clit as if unveiling it for the first time, and Lynn's orgasm—often a shy, elusive thing—burst forth, as bold and strange and miraculous as Sheena's arrival that morning.

PITCHING
A TENT

Emily Bingham

’ll make it worth your while," she says with a wink
as I slip into the driver's seat. Camping was never my
favorite activity, but it's our anniversary so with this
promise, I relent.

The entire trip she's particularly giggly and flirtatious, putting her hand on my thigh and rubbing until
I can feel myself pressing uncomfortably against the
crotch of my pants. Each time I squirm in my seat to
adjust my hard-on she pulls her hand away as if she
enjoys teasing me.

When we finally make it to our sleeping spot—a
wooded area with the flat grassy patch—I'm relieved
to find our site particularly far away from the others,
affording us privacy. From the silence around us, I
can tell we've arrived earlier than the other weekend

campers. I'm thrilled to get out of the car and follow through with what she started during the drive.

The first thing I do is pull Erin to the side of our sedan, pressing her back against the car and kissing her. She's happy to tangle her tongue with mine, moaning and rubbing her body against me. I consider tossing her on the backseat, pulling down her pants and mine for a luscious quickie. Just as I'm about to open the car door, she pulls away.

"Let's set up the tent first."

I'm disappointed but newly motivated when she sneaks her hand into my pants to rub my dick through my boxers. So she wants to continue being a cock tease? That's all right with me; I'll just pay her back later.

Or so I think, as I lay out the tent, surprised it's going so quickly considering the fact that my horniness is making concentration difficult. When it comes time to stake down the tent, however, I can't find the posts anywhere. Looking further, I can't find Erin either.

Frustrated, I follow the trail behind our site. Hearing rustling in the distance, I slow in time to catch Erin pulling off her top; instantly I'm hard. She smiles and finishes undressing as I come closer. When I reach out to touch her, she shakes her head at me.

"It's your turn to get undressed." I do, while she watches.

When I'm finished and reach for her, instead of a handful of my wife's flesh I feel the hard grasp of metal around my wrist, then the click of a handcuff being cinched. Looking at her with shock, I feel the other cuff tighten on my free wrist. Her expression tells me I'm in trouble. I don't know what to say, whether to be concerned or turned on. My cock, stiff and getting more so, doesn't seem to be at all confused.

"Go lie down on your back," she says with a sternness I didn't know she possessed. I notice the blanket she's spread and lie down on it. Erin waits until I'm set before joining me.

"Were you looking for these?" She dangles the tent stakes in front of me, taunting.

"You little..." I start before she shocks me into silence by pulling my arms out straight above me and driving one of the stakes through the chain connecting the cuffs. She smirks as she pulls out a mallet and drives the stake home. My pulse races and I feel sweat beginning to pool at my back. "Honey...?" I start a question I can't finish.

"Shh." She touches her fingers to my lips. "It will be okay. The safeword is Ranger Rick." Her harsh demeanor cracks for a moment as she giggles, but just as quickly she's back in character. I shake my head at her naughtiness and relax as much possible while she shackles my ankles and then stakes them out spread-eagle.

I've never felt so vulnerable and excited. I test the restraints and find she's made sure they're inescapable. Even so, I struggle a bit, having a brief moment of panic as I lose sight of her.

When she returns to my field of vision she's holding a very unsexy bottle of sunscreen. "I can't have you getting burnt. After all you're going to be there for a while."

She starts at my feet and rubs in the lotion, being both thorough and seductive, not missing an inch of my body, except my dick, which she seems to be purposefully ignoring. Cruelly, she even rubs the lotion into the crevice where my thighs and balls meet, making my shaft ache with longing. I groan and buck my hips to convince her to touch me. Instead she sighs with mock sympathy while standing to straddle my body.

From the sheen on her skin I can tell she's already rubbed herself down while I wasn't able to watch. The sight of her so sexy, so close but unreachable is making me crazy. Grunting and trying to pull myself free, I look up at her wet pussy. I'm so desperate I don't dare speak because I know my words would only come out as pathetic begging.

Finally, she squats above me, inches from my dick but not close enough that I can raise myself to reach her. "As for this..." She grasps me roughly in her fist. "We can't let that get sunburnt can we?"

I shake my head frantically and enthusiastically no, desperate for her to stroke me. Instead she holds me in her hand, waiting, enjoying this moment of teasing.

"No, we'll just have to hide it in here." She slides herself easily down on my cock, taking all of me in before pausing to lean down close to my face and whisper, "I told you camping could be fun."

KISSING HEMP INSTEAD OF YOU

Teresa Noelle Roberts

I kiss the hemp rope, coarse beneath my lips and smelling faintly like grass and my own sweat. I do not kiss you, not now. I don't even meet your eyes.

As you wind me and bind me, running rope between my legs and around my breasts, I barely breathe. The rope, and the cuffs you put on my wrists and ankles, are as close to caresses as I'll get for now. Harsh caresses—no fur-lined cuffs and soft nylon rope for us, but steel and hemp.

They make me wetter than kisses on my clit would.

You manhandle me into position, bent over the spanking bench. I go willingly, even gratefully, but you like to pretend to force me and I like when you do so. You tie me down with brisk, silent efficiency, as if you were hanging laundry or trimming the hedge. It's not a rote task like those, but you do it with just as little show of emotion, except that I know your cock is hard, straining against the solemn gray dress pants you wear. No leather for you. On nights we play this way you wear whatever you wore to work, as if dressing up would make this a date instead of the impersonal ritual we both like to pretend it is. Still, your efficient hands are kind, in contrast to the pain they will give me later.

Neither of us speaks. I still don't meet your eyes.

I wind up head down over the spanking bench, ankles and wrists locked in place with the cuffs, torso secured with rope, rope tormenting my breasts and vulva. The position pulls those lines tighter, makes me even more aware of my vulnerability and need.

You stand before me now. I look up, my eyes level with your crotch, which is where you want me. You unzip, grab my hair painfully, force your cock into my mouth. I love to feel you filling my mouth, especially when I'm helpless like this. I'd put it in myself if I could. But you like the pretense of force—maybe need it, though you never admit you need anything—and by now I crave it too. You fuck my mouth as if it's a cunt with more energy and strength than finesse. The lack of finesse is a lie. You know exactly how much force it takes to make me gag on your cock and you push past that point, until I'm half-choking and tears fill my eyes and I'm so wet for you that slickness glides down my inner thighs.

You pull out then, as roughly as you started, and present the cane to my lips.

I kiss it. Then I take the tip into my mouth. When you fuck my mouth, there's no room for artistry or tenderness, but I suck and lick at the cane the way I would fellate you under other circumstances, swirling my tongue on the "shaft" and teasing the "head."

You pull the cane away abruptly, leaving my pursed lips wanting.

I do not meet your gaze. I don't even look at your cock, hard and spit slicked and tempting though it is. I close my eyes so I'm not tempted to watch your feet as you circle behind me. The floor is carpeted, muffling your footsteps.

The first blow of the cane burns and shocks, even though I know it's coming. Slave maintenance doesn't involve warm-up or caresses. No spanks to warm the skin. No love-taps. No touch with anything but the cane, and that touch is an attack.

I scream and thrash against my bonds this first time, hemp and steel preventing my escape, holding me in danger yet safe. The struggle earns me your first word of the session: "Silence!" and another hard blow.

I bite my lip against the pain. Tears well up.

And then the endorphins wash over me as they always do, transmuting the pain to a twisted pleasure.

Fifteen blows in all, each at your full, fierce strength, all but the first in total silence on both our parts. I'm light-headed from pain and desire by the time you bring the cane around for me to kiss once more.

I kiss and suck the cane. I do not meet your eyes or speak or even look at your body, though I'm sure you're still fully dressed except for the hard cock sticking out your fly. You don't speak either, not then, and not when you circle back to slam into me. The fabric of your pants is soft, but it feels like steel wool on my ridged ass, and the spanking bench, though padded, will leave bruises on my hips from the way you're pounding into me. The metal cuffs tear at my skin and the ropes between my legs tug at my pussy lips. Your cock is pounding my cervix, your right hand is threatening to pull out all my hair and your left is bruising the shoulder it grips.

I can barely hold back the orgasm that threatens to spill out without permission

When you come, you utter your second word of the session, "Now!" That's my signal. I come silently, though my mouth opens wide, a scream you will never hear.

You untie me and remove the cuffs with the same efficiency you used to restrain me in the first place. You're still silent, but your touch is gentler than before, and as you help me to my feet, you run one hand down my back.

When you present the rope, I kiss it. I don't look up. I don't meet your eyes.

Then you toss the rope aside and pull me close. "Look at me," you whisper, and when I do I see your sweet smile. "Love you. Love you so much," you say.

"Love you," I answer. "Thank you."

I meet your eyes just before you kiss me, and they are full of tenderness.

TRAIL OF FLOWERS

Sommer Marsden

The banging scared the hell out of me. I almost called the cops until I heard his voice. "Open up, Florence. Hurry."

"Jesus." I threw down my mop and scurried to the front door.

Cathy's Crafts and Classes was small. Very small. And I could hear him pounding like a lunatic. It rattled the walls.

"Hush! Hush! Coming!" I said it all in a violent whisper. The last thing I wanted was to lose this job.

I unlocked the door hurriedly and David pushed inside. "You can't be here!" I said.

"Ah, but I am here." He got up close to me in a blink, pushing me back to the wall. Some blank tote bags, just waiting to be painted or beaded, swung wildly. His kiss was demanding and sweet. Beer scented, to boot.

"You've been drinking."

"Two beers with Mike and Joe is not *drinking*." His fingers skimmed along the top of my waistband, slid higher to cup my breasts. He plucked my nipples through my bra and I shivered despite myself.

"You can't be here," I said again. Though I had yet to convince either one of us.

He shoved my sweater up over my head and then froze. He aimed a finger at the camera pointed our way.

"Fake," I whispered. "We can't afford a real one. But the dummy discourages shoplifting."

He grinned down at me. All wolfish teeth and predatory gaze. "But not public fornication."

I panicked, pushing at him. "David!"

"Shh," he said, spinning me fast. This time I came to rest face first in long garlands of fake flowers. They hung about six feet long so we'd had to tether them from high up on the wall. My cheek brushed faux irises, carnations and daffodils. "It's okay."

"I'll lose my job."

"You won't. All the blinds are down. And your boss is traveling, yes?"

Why had I told him that? But I was wet between the legs and his hands on me were beginning to feel better and better. "Yes," I whispered.

He pushed my jeans down quickly. It was like a magic trick only more startling. Then my panties. He knocked my legs wide and shoved a rigid hand up against my pussy. The hard nudge of his hand to my thumping clit was exquisite.

"See, you like it when I'm all..." He hummed, smacking one asscheek and then the other. "Rough and spontaneous."

Then he laughed. But he was right.

"David. We really should at least go in the back room. I mean, we're right out front and I know the door is locked but...I'm scared..." I was babbling.

"Don't be."

I wiggled to get away from him and he caught my wrists up in his big hand. One hand did the job of trapping me just fine. I saw him reach up and snag a strand of irises dotted with small white flowers. "Tell me, Florence," he growled in my ear. His teeth dragged against my neck and my nipples turned to hard little bits of marble in my bra.

"Tell you what?" My voice was barely there.

"Tell me to stop."

"Stop?"

He chuckled and I felt the bite of plastic against the thin skin at my wrist.

"Are you telling me? Because that sounded like a question to me."

I swallowed hard as he continued to wind the fake flowers up my arm. He was binding me and I was letting him.

"Please," I said. Though I was unsure if I meant please stop or please go.

"I'd love to please you. I wanted to see you tonight. But you had to work. So I'm here now."

He'd dropped to his knees and I realized I couldn't move my arms. I put my head against the wall, let him bend me to his will. I was all in at that point.

He kissed my ass, literally. Dragging his lips and tongue and teeth along my skin until I moaned. My shoulders ached but I barely noticed. I levered myself forward so he had room and he took advantage by pushing his face against me and finding my clit with his tongue from behind. His nose pressed to my ass, his tongue lapping at me so I sobbed.

"Fuck—" I hissed, so close to coming. That fast. Ta-da.

"In a minute." He turned me around to face him. Grinning all the while.

Thick fingers shoved into me, fucked me as he continued to lick. I bit my tongue to keep quiet as I came. Then he turned me again and vertigo swept through me.

I heard his zipper and his rasping breath. "Follow the trail of flowers," he sighed as he tickled the tail of the garland against my asscrack. Goose bumps rose up on my flanks. David bent me forward just a bit more and found my drenched slit with his cock.

"Now the fucking." He pressed his lips against my ear as he started to thrust.

Every stroke pressed my cheek to the swinging flowers, and drove me closer to release. His fingers found my clitoris and he bit my shoulder through my tee.

"I missed you tonight, Flo. Friday night needs you in it. Or me in you."

"I missed you, too," I sighed.

He wrapped his big, warm hand around my throat for the last few strokes. The brief pressure there made my swelling pleasure brighter.

"I'd have brought you flowers," he laughed. "But I forgot."

"That's okay." My cunt gripped up tight around him. I was so close. When he squeezed his hand against my neck one more time, I felt myself tip over into that bright blue bliss of orgasm. I bit my lips as I came. Tasted blood.

"Lucky for us, you had some here," he chuckled. He pressed me to the wall for a few more forceful thrusts as the faux flowers rustled around us, whispering with him as he growled out his pleasure and said my name.

HOSE/TOES

Giselle Renarde

At first it was a little unsettling, being worshipped by two beautiful girls, but Tara and Penn wanted me as their queen. How could I resist?

"Take off your stockings," I commanded from my throne. Those girls looked at me with such reverence it made my heart swell. I didn't need to move a muscle. "Very nice, Penn. Just look at that lovely bush!"

Penn ran her fingers through the honey-gold hair between her legs. "You like it, Queen Keri?"

"I do, my darling. A girl with a nice full bush is a rarity these days."

"Thank you." Blushing, my Penn lifted Tara from her wheelchair. My toes wriggled as Penn laid Tara like a bolt of silk at my feet.

"Good girl," I purred. "Now tie Tara's hands over her head."

"Of course, Ma'am."

Penn's blushing nipples tightened to buds as she secured her panty hose around Tara's wrists. That girl would have stayed put on her own, but she enjoyed being immobilized. Penn laced the stockings around her forearms, crisscrossing nylons over flesh and weaving them all the way to her elbows.

"How's Penn doing, Tara? Too tight or just right?"

"Perfect, Queen Keri."

Penn joined her on the carpet, legs spread, ready to be used. Tara had shaved her pussy, and those bare lips glistened in the dim gleam from the faux-Tiffany lamp. My girls wore nothing, despite the chill in the air. I could wear whatever I pleased, and it pleased me to wear stockings.

"My girls have beautiful pussies." I let my feet hover between their luscious thighs. "Do your pussies love my stockings?"

"Yes," they said. Tara got there first, but Penn was close behind.

"Do your pussies love my feet?"

"God, yes," Tara said.

Penn crossed her leg over Tara's, holding it open. "Please make us come."

"Are you *certain* that's what you want?"

"Yes!" Tara shouted.

I waited a moment, watching as they writhed on the carpet. Their anxiety was electric. I could feel the delicious twisting of their insides, feel their overwhelming heat. My girls were lovely, and they got on so well. They deserved a reward.

Pressing the balls of my feet to their waiting mounds, I rubbed them up and down. My girls squirmed as I stroked them—a bare pussy on the left, a big bush on the right. I plunged my toes into their wet cunts, wiggling inside, collecting pussy juice in my stockings. My girls moaned, seeking ecstasy from my feet.

I would get them off, but slowly.

"Penn," I said. "Lay your naked body on Tara's. I want to watch you kiss her."

Smiles bled across my girls' lips as Penn draped herself over Tara's luscious body. Their soft breasts pressed together. Their mouths met.

"That's right, girls."

I fit both feet between their legs, mashing my heel against Tara's lovely bare lips and Penn's glistening cunt. They gasped together, like one gorgeous entity, before returning to the splendor of their kiss. My girls lost themselves in each other's lust. The queen became extraneous to the scene, merely a tool of their pleasure.

"Good girls." I pressed hard against their pussies, stroking them off with stocking feet. "Very, very good."

SCENT-SUAL

Molly Moore

The smell in the cupboard under the stairs is utterly intoxicating. When I open the door to retrieve my shopping bags it washes over me. Rather than grabbing the bags and shutting the door, I find myself standing there, leaning in a little more than I actually need to and drawing in a deep breath through my nose. It smells earthy, natural, almost like hay. It smells like it looks: coarse, rough, twisted and that neutral color, not white, not gray, not cream, just rope.

I love the rope; even sitting in neatly coiled little bundles in the dark beneath the stairs it draws me into its web of memories and promises. A little shiver ripples through me, excitement, anticipation and memory all twisted up together inside my brain.

I love how it feels against my skin, rough and harsh

but also somehow comforting and safe. When he draws it up through the knots and twists it against my body the friction caresses my flesh with heat as if the rope is almost burning itself onto, no, into my skin. With each added curl he tightens it around me, making me more of the rope and less of me. Sometimes as it gathers closer to itself it will pinch and pull at me, as if exploring my contours and trying to find the perfect fit.

The whole process is slow and methodical, a drip, drip of tension and sensation that my mind slowly falls into as I relax, yield and submit to it, and to him. His focus is unwavering as he guides my body to accept his artwork. I feel like I am the center of everything and yet his eyes rarely look into mine. Instead they study his creation, for in this moment I am created, transformed, into his vision. He is almost silent as he works, concentration etched across his face; there is nothing in his world apart from me, him and of course the cord that binds us to this moment together. There is almost a detachment in his approach to me, as if I am just a toy for him to play with and yet I am also the center of his world.

I am his canvas, empty and clean, waiting to be defiled by the rope. My skin is clear and naked but with each turn and twist of the jute I am slowly transformed and with that transformation goes my mind. As it coils and tightens I relax into it more and more until eventually I feel like I am floating, held firmly by its grip. It is like a constant hug; I feel safe, protected, secure and loved by it. As I let the rope take me my hold on myself is slowly striped away and I become increasingly vulnerable and reliant on him to be in control. Finally when he is done I look down at my arms and legs, admiring the pretty patterns of his work against my skin; sometimes I will pull and tug on my bonds, testing them, loving that unique feeling of them shifting and tightening slightly to hold me just as he has planned. I am caught, trapped, held and exposed to him. He stares at me, adjusts things slightly; he does seem to like things to be just so. The staring makes me fidget for a moment; it is intense and makes me feel so naked, despite the rope clothes that now adorn my frame. For a brief moment I want to hide but then his hands are on me, seeking out the flesh that is still exposed, pulling at me, exploring me; with every touch I am reminded of what I am: his.

Between my thighs moisture pools; I find myself wanting to ask him to touch me there but I have never been very good at asking for it, despite his encouragement for me to do so, and I find myself biting back the pleading words and waiting. His fingers feel cool against the heat of my cunt as he lets them brush past my now-aching clit. I moan, he smiles, the sound of my frustration and longing filling him with pleasure. When, if, I finally get to come my body jerks and twists against the ropes, forcing them to shift around me but never let me go. They hold me tightly in their constant, gripping hug as I breathlessly give myself up to this pleasure.

I can hear my name being called from outside; he

is getting impatient. I only went back for the bags but I have been gone longer than his patience can stand. I reach in and grab the bags, sniffing one last time the scent of memories before finally shutting the door and leaving the house. In the car he watches me as I drive, studying my face and at one point muttering about my flushed expression and the heat of the day, but at the traffic light he leans over and whispers into my ear.

"I know what you were doing, sniffing at the rope. Did you touch yourself?"

I shake my head no.

"Good, because you will tonight, with the rope wrapped around you, the smell of it in your nose and one hand free so you can show me just how much you love us both, the rope and me."

As the light turns green he relaxes back into his seat and watches the world flow past. On the radio there are voices, but I am not really listening, I am concentrating on driving and trying to work out if it is just my imagination playing with me or have the shopping bags brought the smell of their cupboard companions with them?

S

Alison Tyler

The hotel clerk watched the guest waiting. The man had arrived solo about ten minutes earlier and had checked in, gotten his key. Now he sat in one of the deep maroon leather chairs in the lobby. He didn't check his watch. This was what had caught the clerk's attention at first. Most of the "waiters" checked their watches. The man simply sat. He wasn't reading a book, wasn't fucking around on an iPhone, didn't appear to be doing anything except waiting.

The clerk found himself gazing over to the man repeatedly. He felt as if he might catch a statue moving.

When she arrived, the man finally stood. He lifted his wrist, but he didn't glance down the way a person normally would. Instead, he showed the watch face to the woman, whose cheeks flushed. She looked down at the ground, and the man slid two fingers under her chin and tilted her head upward. That simple gesture gave the hotel clerk a raging hard-on, although he had no idea why.

There was heat between these two—the man in the dark-gray suit, the woman all in white. *Almost* all white. She had on a skirt and a tight T-shirt, fishnet stockings, bright-red suede boots with fringe up the back.

The man looked at the boots and he laughed, and that sound made the clerk's hard-on throb. He would have given money to follow them to their room. As it was, he moved quickly around the front desk to watch them enter the elevator together. Before the doors closed, he saw the man push the woman to her knees, her head down, her body completely submissive. He saw that she now had a leather collar around her throat. In the sliver of space as the doors slid shut, the clerk saw that her stockings were visible, fishnets all the way to her toes.

As he was about to turn, the clerk spied a pair of red boots, askew beneath the button to call the elevator.

How he wanted to press that button.

How he wanted to ride that ride.

I'M TIED UP RIGHT NOW

Lucy Felthouse

Nicole pushed the key into the door of her and Steve's house and let herself in.

"Hey, babe, I'm home!"

His response was muffled. "Hi, babe. I'm in here."

She sighed. Even without asking, she knew where "here" was. The damn office. Or, more accurately, the spare room that Steve had turned into a computer geek's wet dream. She'd accepted, when they'd moved in, that it would take a while for him to get things set up. It was his home office, so it had to be right. But unfortunately it had turned into a job that was never finished. Everything was functioning, apparently, but he always seemed to be in there, replacing motherboards, hard drives, adding more RAM—she barely saw him.

Passing through to the kitchen, she put her bag down

on the worktop and flicked on the kettle. "You want a coffee?" she shouted.

"I can't hear you, babe," came the reply. "I'm a little tied up right now."

I'll give you fucking tied up right now, she thought. She'd been a computer widow for months and she was fed up with it. Marching through the house and into the spare room, she prepared to let him have it. But even now, she'd be letting rip to his back. He was under the desk, just his back, bottom, legs and feet visible, and he hadn't a damn clue she was there.

"I said, do you want a coffee?" she shouted loudly, much more loudly than was necessary, and she got an immense feeling of satisfaction when Steve jumped out of his skin and smacked his head on the underside of the desk.

He emerged slowly, then turned and stood, rubbing his head. "Ow. There's no need to be like that. That bloody hurt my head, that did. I might have a concussion now."

She rolled her eyes. "Of course you haven't got a fucking concussion. And it serves you right, anyway. I'm sick and tired of playing second fiddle to all this." She gestured to the leads and components scattered everywhere, then picked up a yellow cable and waved it around for good measure.

"Hey, watch that! It's new."

"Shut up. It's a bloody cable, not a hard drive."

"You could still damage it."

She huffed out a breath, the rage building inside her until it overflowed and forced her to do something about it. Moving over to him, she reached up and slapped his face, hard. While he was still reeling from the shock, she moved behind him and tied his hands together behind his back using the yellow cable.

"W—what are you doing?" Steve sounded genuinely worried, but she knew better. They'd played this game before.

"Sit down and shut up."

"There's nowhere to sit." It was true—he'd moved the chair out of the room as it was in the way of all his junk.

"Then sit on the fucking floor," she barked, a bolt of twisted pleasure coursing through her as he did as he was told.

She placed her high-heeled feet either side of his thighs, so her crotch was in front of his face. Then, not quite knowing what she was doing, or why, she pulled up her skirt and yanked her thong to one side. "Lick me," she demanded. She expected confusion, surprise, refusal...anything that befitted the craziness of what was taking place. But she got none of those things, instead moaning and quickly locking her knees to take her weight as Steve's tongue slipped between her pussy lips.

It had been so long since he'd paid her any attention at all, let alone sexual attention, that she'd forgotten what it was like. But as his talented tongue caressed her slit, causing her juices to flow rapidly, the memories came back. Tangling her fingers into his hair, she rocked against his face, letting the delicious sensations wash over her. Her arousal grew so much that all she really wanted was to come. So she treated Steve like a sex toy, rubbing off against his lips and tongue, pulling him more tightly to her and using him to get her off.

Whether it was the physical sensations or the anger or the situation, she didn't know. But her orgasm hit fast and hard, and she hung more tightly onto Steve's hair to steady herself, taking extra pleasure from the fact that his scalp was probably on fire by now. Her throat was hoarse as she yelled her ecstasy at the ceiling, and it was all she could do not to crumple onto Steve's lap as her climax rendered her limbs jellylike. She managed to keep it together, riding it out until she eventually felt able to move.

Then she stepped away from her husband, pulling her knickers and skirt back into place. Glancing at him, she saw he looked as shell-shocked as she felt. He wriggled, then gave a small smile. "You gonna let me out of this?"

She raised an eyebrow, then lifted her foot and pushed it against his chest until he fell backward onto the floor. "No, I'm not. Not yet. I'm going to make a fucking coffee."

With that, she sashayed back out of the room and into the kitchen, thinking perhaps all those leads and cables weren't so bad, after all. They'd certainly come

TRUSS

Kathleen Delaney-Adams

Trussed with her wrists to her ankles, Kit was forced to angle her body back, her tits upright and thrust forward to receive the lashes. The cool air of the play space, the watchful eyes of the smokin'-hot butch handling the galley whip with such mastery, and her own fevered excitement all served to make her nipples erect and extra sensitive. The butch was not gentle, and each blow landed with such ferocity on her tits that Kit's cunt ached.

A mere hour earlier, Kit had wandered the party aimlessly, pausing now and again to observe a scene. Then hot butch caught her eye, all swagger and confidence. He was sitting against the wall, Levi's-clad legs spread deliciously, working a fifty-foot coil of hemp in hands that a girl just *knew* were strong and capable.

When he raised his head and caught Kit's eye, he winked, then cocked his head in a gesture that was all flirtatious invitation. It was enough to make Kit want to fall over onto her back and open her legs for him without missing a beat.

Instead, she crossed the room and offered herself to him. It was Kit's first experience as a rope bunny, and her heart was as eager for this as her heated pussy was.

Hot butch, whose name she discovered was Trey, was as deft and skilled with the rope as Kit had surmised from watching his hands. His touch on her skin as he wrapped the hemp several times around her hands left her creamy and breathless. When he moved in front of her to cross the rope around her waist, he paused to tug and twist her nipples until she was gasping with pain and pleasure. At Trey's request, Kit knelt before him and leaned back, as he concentrated on tying the rope between her feet. He bound her wrists and ankles together with a series of intricate knots and stepped back to survey his work.

Constrained like this, Kit was completely immobilized and at his disposal. She had never felt so vulnerable, so helpless. She had never felt such desire, such an inferno in her cunt. She shivered with a twinge of fear when Trey stood before her and kicked her knees apart with his boot, exposing her cunt to him. She felt juice on her thighs as his eyes raked over every inch of her flesh. He was pleased with what he saw, she had no doubt, and she felt like a work of art.

Trey pulled the galley whip from his belt loop and teased the air just in front of Kit with it until she nearly came in anticipation. She screamed when the first lash struck flesh, then moaned with longing for more. Her pussy wiggled involuntarily as Trey flicked the whip over it, and Kit's legs opened farther, allowing him easier access. Her own need mounted as each lashed increased in strength until she came so hard she could barely hold herself upright.

Trey knelt on the floor behind her and wrapped his fingers in her curls. He pulled her head back and hissed in her ear.

"I'm not done with you yet."

Kit shuddered.

"Please," she whispered.

"Please?" he taunted. "Do you want more?"

Kit could only nod in answer.

Trey's hands, those strong, masculine, make-a-femme-all-melty hands, moved over her skin, exploring her thighs and the red welts marking her tits. His fingers began loosening the rope, untying first her ankles then her wrists. She burned where the rope had been, and he massaged her swollen flesh with a tenderness that belied the scene they had just shared.

"Good, good girl," Trey murmured.

Kit whimpered and leaned against his chest.

"Open your legs for me."

It wasn't a request, and Kit complied without hesitation. She cried out when Trey thrust three, then four fingers inside her cunt without warning, pumping hard into her slick, aching pussy. Kit rocked against his hand, thrashing wildly on the floor as he punch-fucked her with a hunger that drove her farther and farther into her own desire. She came with a violence that left her exhausted and spent.

Kit closed her eyes and allowed herself to sink into his arms. Moments passed, and she felt the rough touch of the hemp winding its way between her legs and along her belly. Intoxicated by the damp, earthy smell of it, she opened her eyes and blinked dreamily up at Trey.

"Had enough yet?" he asked with a cocky smile.

Her own smile was radiant as she answered, "Hell, no!"

HAND DELIVERY

Heidi Champa

The buzzer went off and I nearly jumped out of my skin. He was right on time. As usual. I walked as slowly as I could manage to the intercom and pressed the button to open the door. I knew it would only take him about a minute to reach my floor, but it was the longest fucking minute of my life. I paced a short line, trying to stay calm to no avail. When his fist pounded on the door, I took the deepest breath I could muster and reached for the knob. Months of flirting and stolen kisses had led to this. I wanted it, but a tiny ember of fear still burned.

Opening the door let in a blast of cool air from the hall, which I was thankful for, as I was already sweating. He stood smiling, his brown eyes cutting through me, his dark hair a mess from the wind. God, he was so fucking cute. In his hand was the package I was waiting for, a delivery from across town that I needed for an urgent project. He stepped closer to me, the smell of him a mix of his familiar cologne and bicycle-chain grease smeared on the leg of his pants.

Instead of handing over the package, he dropped it on the floor, the papers wrapped in a padded envelope hitting the hardwood with a thud. His eyes bored into me and I could hear him breathing hard, as if he'd just ridden up a big hill. Slipping his messenger bag over his head, he briefly looked away as he dug through it and pulled out a chain bike lock, covered in a black fabric. His gorgeous hands wrapped around it and without a word, he took a step, forcing me to retreat one of my own.

When I felt my desk hit me in the back of the legs, he set the lock down and pulled me into a kiss, taking my breath away. He towered over me, his lanky frame more imposing than it looked from a few feet away. Grabbing my wrist, he spun me around with more force than was necessary, which was so incredibly hot. He leaned against my back, his mouth right by my ear, and picked up the lock.

"Give me your other hand."

I did as he asked and the next thing I felt was the smooth fabric over metal against my skin, twining around one arm, then the other. It pinched a bit as I heard the lock click into place. He pushed me forward until my chest was flat against my desk, the weight of the chain resting heavy against the small of my back.

I could hear him moving behind me, the anticipation killing me. I gasped when I felt his hand around my ankle, his forceful grip wrenching my legs farther apart. His fingers slid up the backs of my legs, stopping at the hem of my skirt. It crept up slowly, tickling as the silk lining teased my skin. I shuddered in my pumps when his hand ran over my ass, my thong the only thing left between us. The barrier didn't last long, though, the material gone in a second with one swift yank.

I tested the chain around my wrists: the metal didn't budge an inch. Not that I really wanted it to. Staring at the wall of my office, I groaned when I felt him touch me, one of his thick fingers sliding easily between my wet pussy lips. The tip pressed against my clit, just for a moment, making my eyes flutter closed. Easing my hips back toward him, I felt his finger slip inside me, my body putting up no resistance. His lazy pace was maddening, but I didn't protest; the torment was nothing short of delicious.

"Tell me again what you want."

His voice was deep and sexy, his words almost too much. When we'd talked before about what I'd wanted him to do to me, it was all in the abstract, a fantasy I thought would never come true. It was just talk. But, now, it was real. And I had only one answer.

"I want you to fuck me."

His mouth was once again next to my ear, but he didn't say a word, just nipped at my lobe before disappearing again. The next thing I felt was the sheathed head of his cock rubbing against my wet slit; my body was desperate for him. Seconds ticked by and I had just opened my mouth to urge him on when his hands grabbed my hips and pulled me back, his cock in me to the hilt, forcing the words right out of my mouth.

"Oh, fuck."

He started pounding into me, nearly knocking me off my feet with the power of his thrusts. Then he slowed down, taking his time with each stroke. The chain confining me dug into my wrists but the pain only added to my pleasure. His fingers were back on my clit, moving in small circles, and I felt myself start to lose it. The trembling started in my thighs and soon, my whole body was wracked by tremors, my orgasm roaring through me with an intensity that was overwhelming. The growl he unleashed as he came echoed off the walls, and soon everything was still again. From across the room, I heard the ring of an unfamiliar cell phone, the real world once again intruding on my fantasy.

I felt the chain untangle from around my wrists and he helped me back to standing. Smoothing my skirt back down, I watched as he zipped his pants. He stooped to pick up the package and his bag, slinging the black canvas over his head and back into place. He reached past me, setting the oversized envelope down on my desk. I ran my fingers over the fabric-covered metal where he'd left it and a thought occurred to me.

"Don't you worry about leaving your bike unlocked?"

He chuckled and shook his head.

"Oh, I have another lock. I never use that thing anymore. As a matter of fact, you can hold on to it if you want. For next time. It's too heavy to carry around."

My fingers tightened around the chain as I thought about next time. Before I could say a word, he shocked me by pulling me close and kissing me hard.

"So, will you need a pickup tomorrow?"

I nodded, unable to get out a word. He winked and kissed me again before turning to go, his phone ringing again as he pulled the door closed.

AUDIENCE
OF ONE

Sophia Valenti

The whole scenario had been Keith's idea. His breathless confession came the moment before he climaxed inside me, groaning with abandon. From how aroused he'd been, I could tell that this desire was inextricably entwined with his libido—and before long, it had done the same with mine.

Knowing Keith's sexy secret made me feel powerful, as if I held the key to his very soul. I was touched that he trusted me with his fantasy and put a plan in place to make his dream—and mine—come true.

And that's how my husband found himself naked and bound to a chair by our bed as I lowered myself onto a handsome stranger's cock.

I'd chosen my lover carefully, sidling up to him at the bar while Keith stayed off in the distance, drinking his beer as excitement and jealously coursed through his veins. Whenever I glanced his way, I could see the emotions flashing across his face, warring with each other even as he no doubt felt his cock stiffening in his pants.

Every sweet smile and flirtatious touch I delivered to my new friend was for my husband's benefit. My moves were carefully orchestrated, and I secretly thrilled to the fact that I was turning on two men at once.

Keeping an eye on my husband, I whispered my proposition into the guy's ear. Keith leaned forward at the same time, as if he was trying to eavesdrop on our conversation. From his seat, there was no way he could hear exactly what I was saying, but the script was etched into his heart: *I want to fuck you while my husband watches. He'll be bound and gagged—and forced to watch as I come all over your cock.*

The man smiled before licking his lips wolfishly and letting his eyes flit toward my husband. Keith nodded in acknowledgment, causing the guy to toss some cash on the bar, take my hand in his and escort me to his car.

A short while later, the three of us were in our bedroom. I'd kept the lights on, so Keith wouldn't miss a single detail; keeping the room bright made me feel lustful and brazen. The man hung back while I ordered my husband to strip and then secured him to the chair with soft white ropes. His face was flushed, his cock stiff and tempting, but I resisted touching him. I merely kissed him on the cheek before gagging him, then whispered, "Enjoy the show, baby."

I turned toward the stranger, embracing him as he delivered a brutally intense kiss that made my pussy flood. We stripped each other in a mad haste. Watching this young guy manhandle me had to be making Keith's cock so hard it ached.

I backed my lover toward the bed and tossed him a condom, which he dutifully rolled onto his shaft. As I closed the distance between us, I was mindful of our position. Keith needed to have a clear view of my pussy descending on the man's erection. I wanted my husband to see my juice glossing the stranger's cock—to see every quiver of my body as I rocked through my climax.

Straddling his hips, I slowly slid down onto his shaft, letting him stretch and fill me. I closed my eyes, rapidly rising and falling on that hard, perfect tool. The sound of Keith's muffled groans made my cunt quiver. The red rubber ball gag nestled between his lips may have prevented him from speaking, but not from revealing his exquisite agony as he helplessly watched me take my pleasure from another man. I concentrated on the ecstasy building in me, which grew with each of Keith's garbled outbursts. A grateful sob escaped my lips when I felt a thumb press against my clit, rubbing in firm, precious circles. That sensation was exactly what I needed. I cried out loudly as a man whose name I didn't remember made me come long and hard.

Seconds after my release, he flipped us over. After hooking my legs over his shoulders, he began pounding me hard. As he filled me over and over with his dick, I turned toward my bound husband. The man reared up one last time, his cock pulsing inside me as he climaxed, but I only had eyes for Keith. His face reflected such erotic hunger that my pussy spasmed with a small shimmering orgasm that made me sigh happily.

We slowly disengaged, and the moment my guest caught his breath, I quietly bid him good night. He knew the score and hastily departed after a whispered thanks and a gentle kiss.

Keith was on me as soon as I released him, his hands and lips traveling over my body worshipfully as they traced the path so recently taken by another man. He was drunk with passion, as if we were brand-new lovers, which I suppose, in a way, we were.

The look of absolute abandon on my husband's face as he came inside me was addictive; I needed to see it again. In my head, I was already wondering when we could next play this game—and knowing it would be soon.

MASSIVE ATTACK

Giselle Renarde

Ashanta works weekends. The house feels fucking creepy when Jim's home alone. Too quiet. He snaps on the TV and settles into the baby-blue recliner—a relic from his mother's house, but comfortable as all get-out.

What's that? Is something creaking upstairs?

No, it's nothing. Not a damn thing. House to himself and Jim can't relax, hearing goddamn ghosts in the attic.

Grown man afraid of a creaking floorboard. What a dink.

Wait, there it is again!

A creak. For sure, this time. That's no ghost, no way. Footfalls on the stairs, panther steps, barely there. His muscles freeze. He's incapacitated, can't even turn his head.

And now it's too late. There's a tearing sound, like splitting the seat of your pants, and duct tape wrangles his chest. His heart hammers the dull gray seal. It's a whirlwind as the man in black secures him to Mom's blue recliner.

Some great protector he turned out to be. Thank god Ashanta isn't home. If there's one thing he can be thankful for, it's that his beautiful wife will be spared.

His hands are free, but a lot of good that does him with his arms taped down. His fingers are numb anyway. So are his legs as the guy secures him to the chair, stringing tape round and round the recliner.

The guy...the...guy? The *person*, all in black. The person with breasts. Wow, those are some hefty boobs under that black turtleneck. She's got nice full hips, too. Sweet ass. *Sweeeet* ass. The swell of that big round bottom enlivens Jim's senses. His body comes back to life.

She tears off the end of the roll so briskly cardboard snaps off with the last of the tape. Strutting around the chair, she stands before him, hands on hips. Her black pants fit so snug he can make out a hint of where her pussy splits. Her belly curves like there's one more on the way. And those tits! A huge, heavy swell of flesh sucks him in like a vortex.

But those big frickin' doe eyes win the day. Her glistening lips score a close second. He can't make out any other features beyond the black ski mask.

She leans in, finding his cock and rubbing with the meat of her palm.

"I'm hard," he says.

She smiles, as if to say, *Well, duh!*

The belt comes off, the zipper comes down and she pulls his stiff cock from his pants. Her gloves are so buttery-smooth, and the situation so fraught, that he almost comes right away. He's staring at her tits and that isn't helping matters, so he closes his eyes and takes a deep breath.

His dick pumps precome all over her wrist. He's getting her wet.

Her smile hasn't faded. She sinks to her knees. As she gazes at him like a horny fawn, her fat lips meet his dick. Instead of simply swallowing it, she traces his cockhead round and round like she's putting on lipstick.

"Just suck it, already!" Jim jerks and struggles, but what can he do? He's stuck to the floor. He can't lift the chair. "Come on, please, just suck my dick!"

She raises an eyebrow—he can't actually see her eyebrows, but he's sure she's doing it—as if to ask, *Who's in charge, here?*

Her tongue slides out from between her lips. Pink velvet. He can feel its softness even before the first lick.

She should have taped down his hands. As sensation swirls in his belly like a hot hurricane, the vigor returns to his fingers. He reaches awkwardly for her shoulders and presses them down. The effort pays off, because she licks his dick in sweeping circles, making his cock jerk, making him moan.

Finally, he wins. She consumes his cock like a last

meal. She eats him voraciously, not savoring his skin, but devouring it. The TV blares in the background, and he can't fully shut out the infomercial, even as she sucks his dick.

Her leather gloves leave no prints as they circle his shaft, drawing his attention away from the TV. His erection is wet with saliva, so her fist travels easily up and down his firm shaft. That girl knows what she wants, and she's taking it.

When she smacks his balls, leather snaps against his tender flesh. "Hell, no!"

Hell, yes, she says, telepathically. He can read her thoughts.

Pounding his meat, she sucks him voraciously. Her gloves bring a new level of tightness to the throttle. Hand around dick. Palm hugging balls. She squeezes.

How could he *not* come?

His thighs shudder under the weight of her boobs. Sensation falls out of his arms. If his pulse races any faster, it'll fly right out of his body. No holding back now. He lets go, coating her throat, and she swallows like she loves it. Every spurt. Every shot. She gulps it all down.

When she sits back on her heels, Jim laughs. Utter disbelief. "You gonna cut off all this tape now?"

An impish smirk crosses her lips.

"Crazy woman." He shakes his head and asks, "How'd you get the afternoon off?"

TANGLED

Andrée Lachapelle

The lithe girl hung from the ceiling, twirling, wrapped in blood-red hemp. Her damp hair hid her face from prying eyes, and there *were* prying eyes, and gasps and throats cleared but not one word spoken by the crowd gathered there to watch her spin in the spotlight.

Beads of sweat traveled along her amber skin and stopped at the swollen, darkening places trapped by the harness that had been created as we stood in awe.

A skilled, latex-clad Black Widow had caught the girl in her web.

And not a single one of us longed to free her.

WET NAILS

Ashley Lister

B ondage," Mariah sniffed. She shook her head. "Never tried it. Never will."

She rested back in the seat, extending her left hand to receive the second coat of clear mother of pearl to complete her French manicure. Her lips were pursed tightly, as though the conversation was now closed. She had no interest in hearing about Simon's depraved sexual outlets. Or, to be more honest, she had no interest in letting him know that her curiosity had been piqued.

"It's not for everyone," Simon agreed.

He was the only straight manicurist Mariah had ever met. The others had all been outrageously gay. Simon, dark, attractive and brooding, was unsettlingly hetero with a reputation that suggested he was happy to prove this fact to satisfy the curiosity of any female client. From what Mariah had heard, Simon was able to satisfy more than mere curiosity.

He held her firmly by the wrist. He stroked the polish across each nail with a lazy and languid action. His focus seemed fixed on her hands, his own skill and the aim for perfection with her French manicure.

"I will say," he spoke distractedly, his concentration away from the words, "you don't know what you're missing."

He finished the last nail and smiled for her.

"And you're done."

It was the sort of smile she could imagine him wearing as he thrust into her and allowed his thick, hard length to throb and pulse in a rush of wet, climactic splendor. She tore her gaze away before he could read the lascivious direction of her thoughts. Mariah had no idea where the thought had come from.

She raised her hands and examined the beautiful job he'd done on her nails. The final coat of polish shimmered like molten glass. She held her splayed fingers rigid, as though the very act of moving them through the air might spoil their perfection.

"I'm surprised you've never considered bondage," he mused.

With her hands held by the side of her face, almost as though she was caught in a tableau from a Fosse musical, Mariah considered him warily. "You're really being driven by this bondage interest today, aren't you?"

He shrugged. "You're the one whose hands are currently unusable."

She glanced at her hands, realizing that she was comparatively helpless as long her nails remained wet.

"I—"

She got no further.

He placed a hand on her shoulder, pushing his fingers beneath the lapel of her jacket. She wore only a thin cotton spaghetti-strap top beneath and could feel the skin of his palm stroking against the bare flesh of her shoulder under the jacket.

The contact was surprising, intimate and arousing.

"I—"

Whatever it was she had been about to say, Simon stopped her words with a kiss. His lips, soft yet peppered with the threat of stubble from his five o'clock shadow, pushed rudely against hers. He smothered her mouth with a kiss that was unprecedented, unexpected and divine.

She attempted to reach for him: not sure whether she wanted to push him away or pull him closer. It was at that moment Mariah realized, regardless of her desires, she didn't dare touch Simon for fear of spoiling her manicure. Aware of the limitations of her options, she told herself there were more obvious ways she could possibly surrender to him.

She reached for the front of her jacket, intending to pull open a couple of buttons and expose the skimpy spaghetti-strap top she wore beneath.

Again, the nuisance of her wet fingernails reminded her that, as long as it mattered to her whether or not her manicure looked good, she was unable to resist his advances.

Her heartbeat quickened.

Her pulse raced.

The muscles between her thighs clutched and clenched with warm and greedy anticipation.

His finger slipped from her shoulder and moved down to the front of her top. He hadn't bothered to slide his fingers beneath the fabric. Instead his touch lingered against the thin cotton. The pressure—not harsh yet far from subtle—excited her more than she would have believed possible. Mariah felt the weight of his caress rest over the stiffening thrust of her nipple.

The promise of pleasure was almost enough to make her scream.

When he moved his lips from hers, then took his fingers away from her greedy, wanton flesh, Mariah wanted to sob with frustration.

"It's a shame you've got no interest in trying the bondage thing." He sounded genuinely disappointed. "I'm sure you would have enjoyed it."

And then he was gone, leaving Mariah alone and flustered and desperate and wondering how she could tell him that she might have changed her mind. She decided, as soon as her nails were dry, she would let him know.

NOT BEFORE TIME

Vida Bailey

It's been a long time coming, but I'm finally on my knees for him. My arms are bound behind my back, the soft black rope holds my chest tight. I can feel my breasts presented to him by the harness, thighs apart and taut, messaging excitement to my spread cunt. My urge to be filled is vampiric in its intensity. Where is he?

I smell him draw near. His bare footfalls are soft on the padded floor. His heat is in my face, nearly close enough to touch. Seeking, I reach toward him. I hear the rip of his zipper and the whisper of his cock being taken out. For a second the silky head of it brushes my lips and I whimper as it's withdrawn. He does it again and I strain forward, chasing it with little thought to dignity. I want. Blinded and in pursuit of cock, I'm shameless.

My tongue tags it, once, twice, then it seems I've won because he pushes it home, its blunt head opening my mouth wide. My cunt clenches as I take his length into my mouth, the clean salt tang of him snapping my taste buds, the feel of him familiar hard silk against my tongue.

This time it's different. His hands in my hair aren't rough, exactly, at least not yet, but they're insistent and they brook no hesitation or dissent. This time, I can't move. He claims my mouth, his cock thrusting forward into my throat. My cunt pulses in powerful response but it's too much and I'm slightly horrified at the retching sound that comes from me, at the roll and throw of my stomach as my gag reflex jumps in.

He pulls back and gives me a moment, stroking the hair off my blindfolded face. I breathe, and find my voice. "Damn, Taig. I thought you'd be better at throat-fucking me without making me gag. You know, with all the practice you've had."

He steps back in surprise, startled into a laugh.

"You cheeky slut!"

The slap smacks against my cheek out of nowhere; blind, I get no warning. But it's not so hard. In fact, when he holds the back of my head with renewed resolve and opens my mouth with the thumb of his other hand to slide his cock back in, the smart of it beats along with the blood in my sex and in my tied arms. An ache runs through me and I open my throat to him. I'm harnessed and filled and I swallow him down uncomplainingly. I don't mind the saliva that runs from my forced-apart lips, the noises that come from me, the spit-slick slide of his cock that seems amplified along with my gasps for breath. I don't mind the phlegmy strings of mucous and precome that his thrusts pull out of my throat. He pushes all the way in and holds my face against him and suddenly, my world shrinks to my roped breasts and the way they press against his legs, the dull pain in my crossed arms and the pulse in my clit, the pounding in my womb. I struggle for breath and my head spins, and deep inside I contract in a way I never have before. The breath control, the bondage, his hands on my head—it's all come together in the most unexpected climax.

I writhe against him and he pulls back, worried I'm panicking. Maybe I'm panicking, but it feels like I've moved to a place beyond that. I don't want him to stop but I crumple to the ground, all will gone. I want to sleep. My body feels as heavy as lead and I have no thoughts at all. It's bliss.

Taig squats over me, something like awe on his face.

"I thought you were choking, at first." I shake my head. "But you weren't. You were coming. All tied up, with your throat full of my cock."

"That was my first time blowing anyone dominant," I say, marveling from within my daze.

He sinks to his knees beside me, gingerly pulling me onto his lap. He traces around my breast, from knot to nipple, with delicate fingertips. "You did good, babygirl.

JUST ANOTHER SCOLD'S BRIDLE STORY

Tilly Hunter

Let's get the clichés over with first. Yes, I work in one of those "dungeon" museums full of horrible medieval torture devices and information boards with scenes from the Spanish Inquisition. Yes, we have a little tongue-in-cheek initiation ritual for new staff that involves the pillory. Yes, I'm ordering a custom-made scold's bridle because my mind and sexuality go to strange and dark places.

Phew. Glad that's done. I'll get on with the story in a mo, but I should explode a few assumptions first. I'm not a guide at the museum; I've never made special use of the exhibits after hours; I found the initiation rite funny but not terribly arousing. I'm in the finance office. Borrrrring. I know. But that's how come I've chatted a couple of times to the blacksmith who makes some of our props out in a semi-medieval village in rural Sussex. Nice chap. He fits in our commissions between making wrought-iron gates, reenactment-society armor and bespoke BDSM gear. Which brings me back to the point.

And the point is Tony. My lovely, loving, squeezable husband Tony and his love of imaginative restraints.

I'm on the phone to the blacksmith, Mike. "I need to order one of those scold's bridle things, but it needs to fit someone properly, for, like, a kind of demonstration."

"I see. The ones I've made for the museum are based on actual historical pieces, but when I've had people order them for, er, personal use, we've found they're not terribly effective. They only really work if they're tailored for the, um, user."

"Hmm. Well, I could bring out our, er, willing volunteer to see you. It would need to be at the weekend though. It's not actually for the museum. One of those personal things, as you say."

"Oh, I understand. I could meet you at the forge on Saturday morning."

So off we go, Tony and I, sat-navving our way into the back of beyond one sunny Saturday morning when the hedgerows are frothing with cow parsley and the sparrows are chirruping monotonously, just like they probably did back in the thirteenth century.

You might guess the little misunderstanding that's coming up.

"Have a seat and I'll measure you up," he says, thoroughly non-nonplussed by the presence of sexual deviants in his smithy. But he assumes it's for me.

"No," I say, "it's for him. This is Tony, my husband. Sit down, Tony."

Mike doesn't so much as raise an eyebrow. Tony, on the other hand, is obviously feeling the heat from the roaring furnace. His face is flushed and his forehead damp with sweat. He sits in silence as Mike jots down measurements.

"Could you extend it so there's a collar part too, attached to the headpiece?"

"Sure." He makes the required measurements of Tony's neck while Tony's toes fidget on the dusty dirt floor and the bulge in his jeans cries out for attention. "How do you want it to work? The original version had spikes on the tongue-depressor part. I've made ones with slightly blunted spikes before. Do you want that? Otherwise they can almost always get their tongue out from under it. Unless you make it really long, then it makes them gag and they can't swallow."

We opt for spikes. We go back for the finished product two Saturdays later. This time it's a damp, drizzly day and the yard outside the forge is puddled and muddy.

Mike holds up the bridle for us to inspect. I can't help noticing several sets of shackles hanging on hooks behind him.

"Looking good," I say. Tony says nothing. He's been saying a lot for the past fortnight about how much he's looking forward to trying it on to the point where I thought he was actually trying to provoke me into wanting to shut him up for real. But now he's in the grip of his yin-yang, love-hate of humiliation and there's a lump in his throat stopping him talking.

"We'd better try it," I say.

"I think that would be best," Mike says. And I wonder about him. How do you come to be a twenty-first-century blacksmith making bespoke BDSM gear?

Tony sits and I let Mike fit the bridle, pushing the spiked steel plate into his mouth. Mike is careful to keep Tony's hair from getting caught in the hinges as he closes it and slips a bar of metal over the fastening pin. "You put a padlock on here," he shows me, "and there's space to fit a leash here."

"Can you move your tongue or talk?" I ask Tony.

Garbled noises in his throat and a shake of his head. His hands are clutching the sides of the chair as if he'd very much like them to be tied there.

"And the spikes, they're not too sharp?"

A firm shake of the head.

The metal cage comes down in four strips from the top of his head, the front one dividing around his nose to the mouthpiece before joining again beneath his chin. The separate strip under his chin is a nice touch to keep his mouth closed. The four bars then curve in around the contours of his head to the wide collar. Perfect. I can't wait to get him home. In fact, I'm going to act like a toddler in a shoe shop. "I think we'll leave it on if that's okay."

Mike nods. I pay him and smile as he tells me to

come back if there's anything else I need. What I need right now is to get my husband home.

"Heel," I say to him. I'm mixing my kinky meta-phors, but I can see Mike is impressed as Tony, after just one wide-eyed moment of panic, drops to his hands and knees and crawls to the car behind me through the mud.

WIGGLE ROOM

Rachel Kramer Bussel

That good, honey?" Ned asked, his gaze studying me in all my trussed-up glory. One of the things I love best about my husband is how seriously he takes our bondage play. He's a kinky nerd—the best kind, because he doesn't just like to do things, in bed or out, but to understand why he's doing them. When we got together five years ago, he was a virgin when it came to bondage, discipline, spanking or any kind of power play. "I don't see myself as that macho kind of guy, Yvette," he confessed mournfully to me one night. We've come so far since then.

I've shown him he doesn't have to be what he considers macho to have me at his mercy. I've been there since he took me to a hidden restaurant and fed me all sorts of mouth-melting delights, then went down on me until I came so many times I was giddy by the end. Besides, I'm not into punishment play. He may swat me in the kitchen and tease me for being a "bad girl" because I've burned something yet again, but when he ties me up it's all about getting off.

So instead of being bratty, I simply beamed at him. "Perfect," I replied, which meant that I had plenty of room to wiggle against the pretty purple ropes he'd gotten me for our one-year anniversary. Not only is purple my favorite color, but he'd washed them to make them extra soft and even added little pompoms to the ends so they tickled when they brushed against me.

"Then you're right where I want you," he said. He was a quick study, not needing long to realize that if I was tied up, his tongue could have its way with my pussy until he was covered with my juices. Meanwhile, I could thrash and writhe and feel the sweet tug of the ropes against my wrists and ankles.

"Wait—there's one more thing." I flexed my thighs, straining as I wondered what he had in mind. "I've been reading up on something new." And with that, he proceeded to take a string of red rope and maneuver it around my breasts. I'm a sucker for the feel of rope digging into my skin, but I'm even more of a sucker for a man who takes initiative. The fact that he had come up with the addition of breast bondage made me wet, something he could easily see if he glanced between my wide-open legs. Unfortunately, I couldn't wiggle my way to making sure he felt my wetness; the best I could do was a few upward bucks of my hips, which were met by firm kisses and the instruction to stay still.

"I'll take care of you when I'm ready, don't worry." Soon he was done, and my breasts bulged obscenely against the red ropes. "If I wasn't so eager to play with you, I'd add another one right here," he said, edging one finger along my slit. I stayed as still as I could, lest my eagerness make him focus elsewhere. Instead, I pulled upward against the ropes at my wrists.

I couldn't help a whimper, followed by fast, shallow breaths as I strained against them. My knees kept trying to spread themselves open, but they couldn't go far. Ned traced his fingertips along my wrists and down my inner arms, just enough to lightly tickle me. "Where should I touch you first, my bondage queen?"

"You pick," I said. There were too many parts of me aching for him for me to give an accurate response.

"These look good to me," he said, tugging on one nipple, followed by the other. At first I watched, panting as he twisted both nipples at once, before flicking each one hard with the tips of his middle fingers. When he mashed my now-hard nubs between his fingers, flattening them and causing a current of energy to run deep into my core, I shut my eyes.

"Actually, I can't resist letting you get a little taste of this," he said when he'd given my sensitive nipples a workout. Before I could ask, he was pressing a length of rope against my sex. I strained to get more contact, and he centered his palm against it so it massaged my clit. "There you go; get it nice and juicy." I squirmed against the rope, well aware that Ned was maximizing what little range of motion I had.

"There, I think it's wet enough; let's keep it that way." He took the rope and draped it between my open lips. I sucked on it greedily, staring up at him as he gently stroked my cheek. Ned peeled down his jeans; when his cock sprang forth, I bit into the rope.

"I'm going to undo your ankles, because I want them up on my shoulders." I nodded, even though it wasn't a question. Ned stroked my ankles lightly before hoisting them into place. He rubbed the head of his cock against my wetness, looking down.

Often, Ned likes to tease me, to press his hardness in a few inches, then pull out and simply rest against my hole. Not today. Instead he shoved himself into me, pushing me against our padded headboard. He leaned down, trapping me in a whole new way, my ankles pinned beneath him as he bent his head to suck on my already-ravaged nipples.

And me? I met him thrust for thrust. Sure, I couldn't move much, but that's the thing with bondage—everything is amplified. Every time I confirmed how closely the purple rope encased my wrists, I got that much wetter. When Ned pulled out the next time, he took my ankles and spread my thighs into a wide V. "Wiggle for me, Yvette." With his handles holding my legs in place, I stared back at the love of my life as I did what I consider a kinky dance number—me gliding against the rope, twirling, spinning, showing off. Only I had nowhere to go—except the exact place I wanted to be. I look forward to a lifetime of wiggling, and everything that goes with it.

THE DUNGEON CLUB

Kristy Lin Billuni

At the Dungeon Club, Ceci smiled at Eddie. "So, what are we going to do tonight, Daddy?"

"William's out of town, but Elizabeth is supposed to meet us here," said Eddie.

Ceci winked at Eddie. "That's a whole lotta woman you have to top tonight, big boy."

Turning up a moment later, Elizabeth, a full foot taller than Ceci, had dressed in a tight, sheer, silver slip dress much like Ceci's, and no collar. They exchanged a silent, tucked-chin smile and followed Eddie down a shadowy hall.

"On your knees..." Eddie turned and looked up at Elizabeth. "Both of you." Elizabeth dropped faster than Ceci could. They both bowed their heads, and Eddie walked around behind them. Elizabeth and Ceci waited a long time, listening to Eddie's breathing. "I want you shoeless, tonight, Elizabeth. You're too fucking tall."

"Yes, Sir."

"Daddy," Eddie corrected her.

"Yes, Daddy," Elizabeth said breathlessly, and kicked her shoes off.

"They'll be safe in my duffel."

"Thank you, Daddy."

"Good girl."

Ceci savored a tingle of jealousy and entertained a flash fantasy of a chick fight with Elizabeth over Eddie. The leather collar wrapped around her throat, and she snuck a peek to her right to watch Eddie put another collar around Elizabeth's long, pale neck.

"Ceci, keep your dress on. Tonight you belong to me. Got that?" Ceci nodded. Eddie looked up at Elizabeth. "Both of you. Mine."

"Yes, Daddy," Elizabeth snapped.

Eddie dropped two wooden blocks at the black feet of a cross. "Ceci, stand there, facing me." She—Eddie—tied Ceci's hands up high above her head and spread wide to the two rings on each upper arm of the cross. She tied her feet and the wooden blocks to the lower legs of the cross. Ceci's body stretched taut from her wrists to her propped-up ankles. Her mind whirled. She watched Eddie turn to Elizabeth and tell her to remove her dress and put her arms around Ceci.

Without her shoes, and with Ceci in heels and on blocks, Elizabeth's face rested right between Ceci's breasts. She settled herself into Ceci's cleavage as if she were lying down for a nap. Ceci breathed the sweet scent of Elizabeth's scalp and laid her cheek upon it. They rested there for only a moment before the first strike.

The cross shook with the impact of it, and Elizabeth's knees gave out so that she hung from her arms wrapped round Ceci's waist. Her chin slipped upward, and they caught each other's eyes.

"It's the single tail," she gasped, and Ceci felt both her terror and her glee. Eddie struck her again. Elizabeth stiffened and buried her face again in Ceci's breasts. Ceci looked out toward Eddie, focused, running toward them. Another smack and another fell. Elizabeth pressed into her so that Ceci wished she could cradle her in her strung-up arms.

"Breathe," she cooed. She rested her face on Elizabeth's crown again but kept her eyes on Eddie, magnificent in action. Each blow required a running start and exact placement. Her arm swung with precision, practiced. Each time she raised the red leather whip in the air, her face tightened. Each time the whip landed, her face softened into something angelic, a face Ceci had never seen on Eddie. She glanced down at Elizabeth's back. It looked so long from this perspective and with tiny red beads of blood streaming down against her translucent white skin. The blood pooled, bright red at the top of her round buttocks, then disappeared in the crevice between them.

Their reflection, all three of them in the mirror on

MORNING ROUTINE

Stella Harris

Em sits at the window with an open journal in her lap, a pen in one hand and a cup of coffee in the other. She writes a few words and takes a sip. The process repeats. She thinks about the night before; the hot moments, the tender moments, the exciting moments, and writes them all down. Em thinks of what she might like to do another time and notes that as well.

She absentmindedly reaches her pen hand up to her neck to feel the bite mark on her tender skin; the perfect impression of teeth and the sore flesh around it. She presses into the hurt and her body warms with the memory of the mark being made; the hot lips and tongue that soothed the pain of the bite away.

Soon, she thinks. Soon that mouth will return to her body. Kissing and biting her neck, teasing her nipples, licking her thighs. She shudders and feels wetness growing between her legs. She smiles; even his memory has power over her.

Em takes another sip of coffee and stares at the pages before her. Tries to think of anything else she should note, but loses herself in memories instead. The night before is a blur of sensations, and it takes her a while to tease all the thoughts apart.

"There's ink on your neck." A thumb rubs at her neck as the words are spoken. Before she can react a mouth replaces the thumb, tracing what she imagines is the line her pen left, then finding the bite mark and lining up with it—teeth pressing back into their impression, making her shudder and squeal.

Andrew's arms wrap around her shoulders and his hands reach for her journal, "There's not much writing on that page," he says, teasing disappointment in his voice.

"Maybe I need a reminder," she says, hoping her own teasing will get her in just the right amount of trouble. A growl in her ear is the only answer she gets before she's being dragged away from the window.

She barely manages to set her coffee down as the journal tumbles out of her lap and she's hauled back into bed. What little clothing she'd put on is ripped unceremoniously from her body. Her chest pounds with excitement and just a thread of fear. Her body is sore and used already, and she knows whatever will happen next will hurt.

She knows just as well that it will be the good hurt. The hurt of teeth finding all the dents they've carved out. The hurt of fingers finding all their marks and digging in; hands holding wrists still tender from last night's bindings. And Em's favorite hurt of all, the hurt of Andrew's cock pressing past her already swollen lips.

Her eyes close and her back arches as she gives in to all the things she knows are going to happen, and as she accepts all the surprises she knows are coming too.

She is his to use, and that is the best feeling of all.

BOUND

Jenne Davis

It had been a week since they had last talked, or rather she had screamed and he had just stood looking as guilty as he was. A week ago the idea of even seeing him ever again had been out of the question. His stupid indiscretion was going to cost her everything, everything that she had worked so hard to preserve over the last five years. Her marriage and her standing in the community. The shame of knowing that her best friend had been the one who had tempted him away from his dutiful loving wife had filled her with more rage than she thought she was capable of ever feeling.

She was damned if she was going to forgive either of them. The only reason she was back in the house was to pick up her things, and he was not supposed to be there. He should have been at work, but he wasn't. Instead she found herself in the one room in the house that she truly loved, facing the man that she thought had truly loved her.

"What the hell..." she began to ask, her voice quivering a little, her composure almost gone at the sight of his disheveled face, his shirt unwashed. She couldn't recall a time she had seen him unshaven, basically broken. "I came to get my stuff..." It was all she could think of to say, and yet, as the words left her mouth she felt an immediate pang of regret.

"I...I'm sorry," he blurted out.

Thoughts came flooding into her head as she watched him, his head bowed as a monk in penance would be, now silent. The powerful man who was always in charge of himself and those around him, wasn't anymore. He was broken and for some reason in that moment, she felt the need to fix him, to be the one who took control, the strong one... More than that she realized that she needed to repossess him; he was hers, and giving him up was suddenly unthinkable.

They looked at each other, neither daring to move, but both straining invisibly to touch the other. "I'm sorry...you have no idea how sorry I am. Can we fix this? Can you help me fix this?" The desperation was all too clear in his voice as the words left his mouth. "I want you in my life, and only you."

The tension was palpable as they grazed each other's bodies, running their gaze up and down, neither daring to make the first move. She broke the spell and moved closer. Reaching out and touching his chest, reveling in the sensations as her hand began to roam across the cool cotton.

He returned the favor and she felt his hand brush her neck and it was then that the floodgates of desire began to open. Before he could touch her further, she purposely unbuttoned his shirt, allowing herself to feel a brief rush of excitement as it dropped to the floor. Then with one swift movement she was on her knees.

She looked up and met his gaze. She could see and feel the want in those smoky brown eyes. Slowly she unbuckled his belt and popped his fly button. She undid his zipper, her eyes fixed on his. She ran her tongue around her lips, as she tugged at his pants until they lay on the floor. His boxers were peeled from his body, his prick released liked a spear, and she could resist no longer.

Eyes still locked on his, she began to lick not just her lips but also his cock. Long licks ensued as she teased him, waiting for him to beg her for more. His eyes spoke much louder than his voice ever could as suddenly he was devoured, slowly but deliberately. Taking him. Tasting him. Bringing him to the edge but never quite letting him get there. Over and over again. His eyes pleading with her to release him from the spell her mouth had over him.

The surge that passed though her was like that of a power grid lit up by a lightning bolt as she finally allowed him to spill into her mouth. The pulsing sensations that passed over her lips were distinct and she knew that he would not stray again. Continuing to look into his eyes, she enjoyed the salty taste that hit her throat, swallowing deeply, allowing the feeling of power to wash over her.

Releasing him, she knew that once more they were invisibly bound to each other. This was one bond that simply could not be broken.

DOUBLE DARE

Annabeth Leong

I dare you to make yourself come," Dylan said, his features made boyish by the schoolyard tone of his voice. Neither of them had bothered to get dressed yet, and his soft cock gave a friendly bounce as he strode into the room holding one cup of coffee.

Alexa snorted and stretched, enjoying the slide of sheets against her skin. She had no trouble pleasuring herself under normal circumstances. "What's the catch? And why didn't you bring me a cup?"

He tossed a length of rope onto her bare stomach.

"I see. You want to be a teasing bastard."

"Pretty much."

She fingered the hemp, grinning. "Am I crazy if I think this sounds like a perfect way to spend a Saturday?"

He kissed the end of her nose. "You think it'll take

all day to make yourself come?"

Alexa stuck out her tongue, not quite fast enough to lick his chin. "I know my husband, that's all."

"Yes, you do."

They started with a hog-tie on the bedroom floor, but Dylan really cranked it. Alexa, glad for all the yoga she'd practiced, wound up in a bow position, so her stomach was the only part of her that touched the ground and her back curved in a deep arch. He supported her knees and shoulders with carefully placed pillows, but it didn't take long for Alexa to discover the dark side of the seemingly considerate gesture.

Dylan placed her favorite vibrator on the floor between her legs, switched on and just centimeters away from her suspended clit. The pillows limited her range of motion, so she couldn't rock her body to press against it. By pushing hard against their soft restriction, Alexa could just brush her nipples against the carpet, or touch her clit lightly to the vibrator. All that got her was a delicate buzz that aroused her but did nothing more.

She growled, and he laughed. Then she inadvertently knocked the vibrator out of place with her struggling thigh and let out a desperate howl. Dylan gathered her bound body tenderly against his chest. "Sweetie, you're the best."

"God, you're awful."

"Here, I'll help you out." He slipped his hand under her body and offered his palm. Alexa considered stubbornly rejecting this, but couldn't really manage to resist his firm, calloused skin. She rubbed against him shame-lessly, the beginnings of her orgasm gathering with a shimmering glow behind her eyelids.

He pulled his hand away at the last possible moment. "I. Dare. You."

"You dare me to what?" Alexa wailed. She rocked as much as she could and struggled in his arms and ropes. "How am I supposed to come if you won't let me?"

"Poor thing," Dylan answered with mock sympathy. He retrieved the vibrator and moved around behind Alexa, where he traced delicate circles around the entrance of her cunt with the very tip of it. She almost sobbed.

"Please…"

"You're so wet. This must be awful for you."

"Put it on my clit, damn it."

He shoved it into her cunt instead, and it slid in deep because she'd gotten so wet. The vibrations made her ache deliciously, but they would never make her come from that position.

"Dylan, I'm warning you."

He chuckled.

"You have no idea what teasing even is."

"I can't wait to find out." He substituted his cock for the vibrator, and tangled his fingers in the web of ropes that held her in place. He fucked her, using her body like a lever and fulcrum, like a simple machine made for pleasure.

She gloried in how he filled her, but she needed more if

she was going to come. "Where did that vibrator go?"

"It must have rolled under the bed."

His strokes came faster. He panted like he might come soon. Alexa wasn't sure if she should beg him to slow down or give up and moan.

Then, abruptly, his cock withdrew.

"Oh my god," she whispered.

"How are you going to make yourself come?"

Alexa's desperation transcended Dylan's dare by now. With little grunts she rocked and wriggled on her belly until she managed to get one of his pillows between her legs. She closed her eyes, threw her head back and rode the pillow.

Her hips moved with sharp little thrusts. She forgot everything—the ropes, Dylan's eyes on her body, the threats she had been making.

Then Dylan yanked the pillow, too, out from under her. Alexa screamed, so frustrated that she didn't realize at first that he'd replaced it with his face. Adrenaline and arousal gripped her. She pressed against his lips mercilessly, wanting to drown him in cunt juice, wanting to come so hard he felt it in his teeth. He gave her his tongue, slid one finger slowly up her cunt and circled her asshole with a thumb.

She gritted her teeth and rubbed against him harder. His thumb slipped into her ass up to the first knuckle.

Finally, explosively, Alexa came. Dylan began to slide away from her, but Alexa growled, "Get back there. I'm not done."

He twisted his head to the side to free it from her cunt. "Hey now. Who's the one who's tied up?"

She laughed. "You're the one who dared me and got me wound up like this."

"Mmm. True." Dylan returned his tongue to her clit. Alexa enjoyed the sensation and fantasized about the double-dog dare she'd soon send his way.

She could sense him nearby, feel his protective presence as she was groped and fondled by strangers. He had been the one to secure her wrists to the suspension cuffs, tightening the restraints until he felt assured they would not slip nor cut off her circulation. The bite of the leather on her flesh and his warm, strong hands on her had made Delilah dizzy with desire for him. Agonizing, wanting only him, her exposed flesh offered for the pleasure of others.

She nearly cried out as someone began to torture her up-thrust tits, twisting and pulling on them, slapping them with their hands and then with what felt like a paddle. Delilah writhed in the air, the suspension creaking as she strained against her restraints, her observers taunting her and shouting their approval. When her torturer took her nipple between his teeth and bit down hard, her body froze in pain. When he released her raw tit, she sagged in midair, held upright only by the leather cuffs. She panted quietly, fighting to return her breath to the slow steady inhale, exhale she knew from experience would get her through this scene.

Delilah felt hands on her heated flesh, working her over, several pair at once. Her thighs were spread open and her clit flicked hard with a finger, again and again. Juice splashed out of her cunt, onto her legs and the hand that fondled her, but still she did not come. Someone was massaging her breasts, almost tenderly, playing lightly with her sore nipples. Delilah arched her back, forcing her tits farther outward, hungry for more. She was shivering uncontrollably, unaware that tears were silently trickling down her cheeks.

Tender hands traced Delilah's skin, running slowly up her side, caressing her shoulders, moving over her stretched arms, as if savoring every inch of her flesh. She sighed and shuddered deliciously. She felt someone unfastening the restraints that bound her aching, bruised wrists. Several pairs of arms held her upright, then lowered her to the floor gently. Her wrists were massaged and soothed. Once the blood flowed back into them, they began to throb in earnest.

Abruptly, Delilah's arms and legs were grabbed and pulled apart. She was stretched opened and held down. Although she struggled for several moments, she was unable to move, such was the strength of her captors. She gave in and lay still, holding her breath. She knew her pussy was exposed, her entire being on display. The thought saturated her cunt. She wiggled it without thinking.

"Don't move," someone hissed. She ached to rock her hips, her pussy, get some relief from the need coursing through her. But she obeyed.

The room was completely silent, not a sound save Delilah's hoarse breathing. Where was Von? She couldn't hear anyone, and her eyes remained dutifully closed. Was he still watching her? She could feel eyes on her thighs, her skin. Feeling completely helpless, she wanted to close her legs, roll over and hide her nakedness.

Someone grabbed her hips, raising her ass off the

floor and into the air. A sudden deep thrust, and she was filled with cock, a cock she recognized instantly as Von's.

He pumped into her tight pussy, fucking her hard and without lube like he always did, and Delilah responded in kind. She rocked and rode his cock, moaning softly and struggling again against the hands that pinned her arms and legs. Her back arched as she received him, thrust after jackhammer thrust, crying out with pleasure, until she could no longer even move from exhaustion. She lay panting beneath him when he pulled out. She felt his come splash onto her tits and stomach.

Delilah's arms and legs were released, and there was a spatter of applause from the small crowd. She stretched luxuriously, basking in the aftermath of what would go down in her memory as the hottest scene of her life.

She opened her eyes and peered up at Von's face.

"Von? Von, did I please you?"

Von chuckled with appreciation, and leaned down, his mouth on her ear.

"Yeah, you pleased me. Happy birthday, baby," he whispered. "Would you like to come now?"

Delilah's smile of anticipation was all the answer he needed.

GOING DOWN

Sacchi Green

B ent over my lap, bound in gorgeously intricate rope-work from tits to tush and thighs to knees, Kiki still kept stealing little peeks at the onlookers. I swatted her extra hard where the binding framed the reddening expanse of her ass. "Kiki!"

"Yes, Ma'am! Sorry, Ma'am." Memorized lines. No genuine submission. Even when pinches got her to the point of tears she still played to the audience. Not topping from the bottom, but close. You can lead a girl to sub space, but you can't make her sink into it if it's just not her nature.

Well, we'd negotiated penetration, too, so all right. The snap of my latex glove did get her focus back where it belonged. She responded like Pavlov's dog, though drooling from quite a different orifice, and wriggled her ass upward as much as she could. I kept up the spanking until moisture gleamed between her thighs, then slid two fingers into where she needed them most. She'd wanted more than two but hadn't earned them. Still, when my other hand squeezed underneath to work her clit, she plunged as deeply into the moment as my fingers did into her, and her bound body rocked across my lap in time to very genuine cries and moans.

In the aftercare space, Toni, the rope artist, carefully loosened her handiwork while I soothed the minor welts on Kiki's skin. "So how did you like performing in public?"

"That was amazing! Except..."

Toni's eyebrows shot up. I just shrugged. "Except what?"

"Except nobody was, well, shocked or anything. I wish...um, I wish, Ma'am..."

"Shocked? At a Fetish Fair play party?"

She just looked up at me with big puppy-dog eyes. "Well, what do you wish?" I said, relatively mildly. Like pain pigs, performance pigs do have their place.

"I want to be really, really depraved! Enough to make some old biddies hopping mad!"

"And get away without having to post bail, I assume."

From her blank look, she hadn't thought things through that far. Ah, youth.

Toni struggled not to laugh. I knew what she was

thinking. We'd been involved in some pretty dicey capers in the past. "No old biddies here," she said. "Nobody to get their panties in a twist, if they're even wearing any. But something might be arranged."

Kiki looked interested.

"You don't get sick in elevators, do you, kid?" I asked. Kiki shook her head.

"Not tonight." Toni passed the rope to her boi Syl, who coiled it neatly. "Give it a rest. If you look okay by tomorrow night you can be my model for the ropework demo. If you're very good and obedient, you might even get a reward."

By the following night Kiki's rope welts had healed nicely, and she proved to be a very, very good demo model. Afterward, buttoned into a coat with just her lower legs freed from the ropework and hands bound behind her, she followed us meekly with tiny geisha-like steps to an elevator.

At the top floor Syl held the door open to stall the car while Toni whisked off Kiki's coat and helped her kneel, positioned so that viewed in profile from the door the ropework down her torso and up her thighs accentuated the peach-round curve of her ass.

"Last chance to back out," I said.

Kiki looked up, saw what I'd just pulled down across my eyes, and caught her breath. A Fetish Fair crafts dealer sells demonic leather half-masks right out of the commedia dell'arte. I have quite a collection. "Extra shock value. Makes me extra mean."

Dealers sell a wild array of silicone cocks, too, but my special-occasion model, with an oriental dragon's head at the tip and a subtle pattern of scales along its length, was handcrafted in Shanghai. When I pulled it out Kiki looked down, and with barely a pause—and without asking permission—saluted the dragon with a flick of her tongue. If only such talent came with a submissive spirit!

"Let 'er roll!" Syl and Toni stepped back into the hallway. The door closed. I pushed the button for five floors down.

Kiki worked my dragon with tongue and lips, worshipping every ridge and swirl, maybe imagining them, as I was, in her hungry cunt instead of her mouth. I hadn't intended to be turned on, but my insides lurched as the elevator dropped. My hips thrust toward her so hard she had to pause to get her balance, bound as she was, and as the car jolted to a stop I grabbed her head to steady her.

The door opened. The crowd outside erupted in gasps and raised voices and a scream or two. Kiki tried desperately to look at them out of the corner of her eye while I kept a vicious grip on her hair with one hand and punched the CLOSE button. The sliding door nearly trapped an outstretched arm draped in a nun's habit. Then I hit the button for the sub-basement, and Kiki got right down to hitting my own button with the base of my raging dragon cock.

By the time Toni and Syl caught up—or down—with

us, Kiki and I were both sprawled against the side of the elevator and gasping for breath.

"Fantastic organization, guys," I said when I could speak. "The nun was a brilliant touch." Kiki only looked startled for a second or two.

"The gang had a great time helping out," Toni said, beginning to loosen Kiki's bonds, "but it looks like you had an even better one. Gets mighty hot when you rub two performance pigs against each other."

Kiki glanced at me slyly. "I wish, Ma'am," she said, "that we could do that at Macy's. Or the Empire State Building."

"Don't push your luck, kid." But wheels were already turning in my mind. You never know.

SWITCHING
IT UP

Heather Day

Nicole suppressed a gasp as the leather cuffs snapped closed, and wondered, not for the first time, if she could really do this. Ben had convinced her that she'd enjoy it once they got going, but she felt tentative and vulnerable and, just for a moment, seriously considered using the safeword.

She was just so unused to being the dominant.

Looking at Ben's naked body, wrists cuffed around the bedstead bars and ankles shackled, she remembered fondly all the times it had been her in that position. All those times she'd just been able to let herself melt away as Ben's fingers, mouth and cock took them both on a journey to dark, undiscovered lands. He was just so goddamn good at it, it had never occurred to her to switch.

Until, that is, he'd made the suggestion, with *that* look in his eye and she could tell that the idea turned him on. So here she was, in her finest lingerie, trying to figure out what she should be doing and ignoring the butterflies in her stomach.

She positioned herself on all fours above her man and took a moment to contemplate his body. His hard, tanned chest, the fuzz of his exposed underarms and of course, his magnificent, ever-ready cock…

"You're not to talk unless you have my permission, got it?" At least she sounded dominant, even if she didn't quite feel it yet.

He nodded. Now, what might he enjoy? No, that was the wrong question. How might she use his body for her pleasure? Nicole smiled, suddenly realizing that after all the nights he'd spent subjecting her to spankings, teasing her clit with vibrators and cruelly withholding the release she so badly needed, the power was now all hers. Her nerves subsided; it was time for payback.

She started by running her fingernails lightly over his chest, enjoying the way that he flinched at this simple action. His body was tense, primed for sensation. She knew that feeling well. Nicole lowered her head and flicked, slowly and repeatedly, at his right nipple with her tongue—an action that he'd never been too keen on. With her right hand, she pinched and squeezed his other nipple, causing it to pucker and harden. Ben made a small, interesting noise and her pussy clenched in response.

"Aw, not enjoying yourself?"

She was surprised by the taunting glee in her voice, but happy in the knowledge that he could make it all stop with one word if he really wanted to.

"Now, what shall we use on you?"

She surveyed the impressive collection of toys lined up next to the bed and picked up an anal plug. "This?" Discarding it, she then picked up an unforgiving pair of nipple clamps. "These?" His eyes widened even further. "How about this?" "This" was the fiercest bullwhip they owned. She had no intention of using it, but it was fun watching Ben squirm in his restraints when she was used to seeing him so calm and controlled.

"Close your eyes."

She fastened a soft, purple blindfold around his head, knowing how much that would heighten his anticipation of what was to come.

Quietly, she reached down to the side of the bed and opened a small wooden box from which she retrieved a gleaming metal instrument. The Wartenberg wheel. Although it looked ferocious, the sharp-pronged wheel could actually convey all manner of sensations, from sharp pressure to a light tickle.

It was the lighter end of the spectrum that she utilized now, running it delicately up Ben's thigh, across his stomach and chest and toward his exposed underarm. Ben was twisting his body this way and that, trying in vain to escape the path the wheel was trailing across his skin and no doubt realizing that Nicole was heading for his most ticklish spot. When she reached it, he flinched in so endearing a manner that she decided to spend some time tormenting his sensitive underarm skin with her nimble fingers. When she'd had him half laughing, half gasping for several minutes, she decided that the poor boy had earned at least some reward.

Nicole lowered herself down his body and took his cock all the way into her mouth. Ben responded with a loud, relieved moan and the tiniest of hip thrusts. A feeling of pure power coursed through Nicole and inflamed her already-tingling clit. She worked his penis around her mouth and massaged his balls, encouraging him on to orgasm. She listened carefully as his breathing got heavier, felt his cock get even stiffer, and just before the pivotal moment arrived, she stopped.

Ben howled. A desperate, undignified mixture of pain and frustration. She'd made the same noise many times herself.

Nicole stripped off her knickers and straddled his leg, her juices coating his skin.

"Feel that?"

He nodded. She started to grind her pussy against his leg.

"That's what you want, isn't it? You may answer."

"Yes." His voice was small, chastised.

"Well, I might just let you have it. But first, I'm going to make myself come. And you're going to watch."

She took off his blindfold to reveal desperate eyes that were instantly fixed on the movement of Nicole's hand; two fingers inside herself and thumb working her clit. His cock was twitching, desperate for attention.

"Oh yes—oh!" Nicole came triumphantly, head thrown back, making a big show of it for her captive audience. Ben moaned softly, sounding broken.

"Please," he said, "may I come now?"

"Hmmm," said Nicole, "I think I'm going to make you wait a bit longer, for speaking out of turn. Besides, there are so many toys I haven't tried on you yet."

She smiled a wicked smile at him, drenched in post-orgasmic bliss, and went to choose the next object of torment.

Guess I do have a bit of a dominant streak after all, she thought.

way his even, measured breaths grew more erratic and ragged. That subtle cue let me know he was as turned on as I was. Those zen-like moments where he makes sure the ropes are positioned with perfection are our foreplay.

Once he was satisfied, Elliot stood back to admire his work. His heavy gaze was like a teasing caress that made me more desperate to have his cock inside me. I squeezed my thighs tight, grateful he'd left my ankles unfettered, and felt arousal welling inside me. I began to squirm, my patience quickly running out, and parted my legs in invitation.

Elliot can never resist me for long. His cock, hard and tempting, bobbed in front of him as he climbed onto the bed. I arched upward and tugged on the ropes, moaning with delight as I felt the burn surrounding each of my wrists. My cherished bracelets of fire. Elliot wrapped his arms around me, supporting my back and mouthing my breasts. He tongued each nipple in turn as I tried to grind my pussy against his pelvis. His cock was so temptingly near, but with my hands secured there was no way I could force him inside me. I was at his mercy, and my heart raced wildly with ecstatic desperation.

My moans rose in volume, and Elliot answered my wordless call. Bringing his lips to mine, he kissed me fiercely, his tongue taking possession of my mouth as his cock drove inside me. I was overwhelmed by sensations, eagerly letting every care slip away. My entire world was reduced to the feeling of his cock plundering my pussy and the intensity of his kisses stealing my breath.

I wrapped my fingers around the rope that criss-crossed my palms as Elliot pumped into me harder and faster. He moved his hips in a sexy corkscrew motion that kicked my arousal higher each time he made contact. I lifted my hips as high as I could, inviting his thrusts. The pain, the pleasure and my utter surrender washed over me in a sensuous wave of orgasmic bliss. But when the rapture faded, I knew the burn would linger, and I smiled.

SEVEN KNOTS

Tamsin Flowers

When I look up, he's standing in front of me, gazing down at me with a passive expression on his face. He doesn't speak. In his hands is a skein of coarse blue rope, not thick, but rough and fibrous. He hasn't tied me with rope before; he's only used leather cuffs and belts to restrain me so far.

I hold out my wrists to him, supposing this is what he wants, but he shakes his head. Instead he simply points toward the heavy mahogany table that dominates the center of the room. I climb up and kneel on the table as I've done so many times before, leaning forward to rest my head on my folded arms. He moves almost silently across the room, but I sense his shadow falling on the polished surface of the table.

"Do you know what Shibari is?" he says.

I look up and shake my head.

"It's an ancient Japanese bondage technique. Release through restraint."

He starts to unravel the rope. It smells like garden twine and there is a pleasing slapping sound as he lets one end drop to the floor. A small whisper of desire starts to unfurl inside me.

"Each of the seven knots I'll tie will represent both reward and punishment," he says. "Kneel up."

He gathers my wrists together behind my back and winds the rope around them several times. Then he pulls the end of the rope up through the narrow space between them. The friction of the rope burns the fragile skin. He knots the rope.

"This first knot is punishment for the times you have touched me without my permission."

He yanks it tight, pulling my arms back hard until I can feel a searing tightness across the front of my chest. And a sharp twist of desire, hot and high in my vagina. He brings the two ends of the rope around to my front, winding them twice around my waist before he ties the second knot. It's more complicated than the first, but this time he doesn't rip the rope across my skin as he tightens it.

"This knot is reward for the beauty you bring to my life; for your white skin and red hair, the soft curve of your belly."

His hands brush my skin as he threads the ends behind the knot; he lets his fingers linger where the flesh rises from my stomach to my mound of Venus. My legs tremble. A whispered sigh escapes my lips.

He uses one hand to spread my knees, then he draws the two lengths between my legs, allowing each to settle in the creases at the top of my thighs. He pulls the ropes tight, up between my buttocks, and I feel him securing them where my wrists are tied at the back of my waist. The pressure cuts deep, almost bisecting me. I'd never realized it was a feeling I needed, this tight, sawing friction.

"The third knot is to remind you that certain parts of your body are in my possession."

It's not something I could forget.

He goes to the shelf in the corner and picks up another rope, this one red. He twists it around my back and over my shoulders in three figures of eight, each twist and turn trapping my breasts, constricting them until I'm sure they'll burst. My nipples throb and pulse for the slightest touch of his hand but he works carefully, encapsulating the soft white orbs without ever touching the dark areolae.

A cry sits silent in my throat. I want to beg for the release he promised. But this is only the fourth knot he's now securing at the center of my breastbone.

"This one is punishment for your pride," he says. "Only I can be proud of your breasts. You must be humble."

With the fifth knot he binds my ankles with a black rope, twisting it around the narrow joints until they burn. Scorching pain marks my skin and blossoms up through me like a flame.

"This will remind you never to run from me," he says through gritted teeth.

He's referring to the time I tried to leave him, to break my addiction. I came crawling back on my hands and knees. He's the only one who can give me what I crave and he doesn't need to shackle my ankles to keep me bowed at his side.

The black rope is long. He draws it up to my waist and secures it to the large knot at my belly. The sixth out of seven.

"Your loyalty will be rewarded soon," he whispers in my ear.

He lowers me gently onto my back and pulls the black rope tight, feeding it through the knot as he does so, until I have bend to my knees up. He keeps pulling it through until my heels press against my buttocks. My hips jerk, pushing up to make my needs known.

"Not yet," he says.

I watch as he ties a large, intricate knot at the end of the rope.

"This seventh knot will be your reward," he says, when he notices me looking at him.

He holds it up and I see a bulbous black knot, scratchy and fibrous. He slips the fingers of his other hand between my legs.

"I knew you would be wet. You always perform for me, don't you?"

Spreading my legs, he inserts the great knot into my vagina, pushing it up hard, thrusting it up and down against the soft flesh inside. My body bucks against the constraints as I come, pulling the ropes tighter and tighter until they set my skin on fire.

"Embrace the ropes," he says, "and you'll find your release."

As my orgasm continues to blossom and burn, he turns on his heel and leaves me alone.

HURT ME, SIR

Sophia Valenti

The sound unraveled me, perfectly and completely. That clink of steel against steel as Jason rummaged around in his nightstand drawer for the handcuffs. I think he knew what that noise did to me, because he jostled the cuffs more than necessary before he pulled them into view. By then, my cunt was absolutely aching.

I was already gripping the curlicues of his brass headboard. He'd ordered me to hold my hands over my head, while he'd lavished my breasts with long, wet kisses that he interspersed with sharp nips of his teeth. With each burst of pain, I raised my hips upward, my body begging for more of his touch.

"You stay put, bad girl," he murmured, his sly smile making filthy promises I longed for him to fulfill.

Having him direct me to hold my position made my

pussy grow hot and slick, but when I'd heard that unmistakable metallic clang, a fresh wave of arousal washed over me. I was a humming ball of sexual energy, waiting for the moment when those twin bracelets of steel would encircle my wrists in their unyielding embrace—and knowing that was only the beginning.

Without delay, Jason fastened a cuff around one wrist and then the other. The satisfying snick delivered by each lock made my pussy even wetter, and the cold steel against my skin made me shiver—but my response had nothing to do with the temperature. Jason lifted the chain between the cuffs, jerking my wrists higher as he threaded the chain through one of the hooked flourishes on his headboard. I tugged my hands to acknowledge what I already knew—that they were tethered neatly. Sure, I could have maneuvered my hands and unhooked the chain with some effort, but where would be the fun in that?

I was his captive because I wanted to be. That tacit acknowledgment of my submission made it that much sweeter—for both of us. I trusted him enough to bind me and take his pleasure, just as I trusted him to give me what I needed, too. In surrendering to his will, I always found a peaceful clarity, much like I'd ultimately find pleasure in the pain he never failed to deliver.

Jason's eyes shone with a predatory gleam that made my pulse quicken. His gaze was intense as it raked over my body and honed in on my nipples—pebbled and damp from being worked over by his tongue and teeth.

Jason slipped between my parted thighs, his hard cock riding the length of my slit. He was so agonizingly close but not penetrating me as he pinched my nipples fiercely. I gasped as the sensation wracked my body, and Jason's response was to release my breasts and jam his cock inside me. His smile let me know how much he liked this game, so I wasn't surprised when his beautiful torture cycled in an endless loop. He'd pull out of my pussy, only to abuse my nipples and then reward me with a stroke of his cock for accepting the pain.

As he continued to tease me, my eyes filled with tears I could barely contain. Even so, I longed for the next wicked spark in order to feed my sexual hunger. I was hovering on the edge of climax; it was so close I could barely speak. I knew what I needed: one more thrust of his cock, one more twist of his hips to grind his body against my clit.

"P-p-please," I uttered in a whisper as Jason's cock rested against my pulsing clit.

"Please what?" he answered, cool and removed in a way I could never be. I was nearly coming apart at the seams, sweaty and teetering on the brink as the hand-cuffs' chain made sexy music by clanking against the headboard while I writhed in desperation.

I released a soft sob, and my eyes fluttered closed before I managed to say, "Please...hurt me, Sir."

"Oh, you heartbreaker," he responded, his voice low and hoarse.

Jason did what I asked, giving my nipples one last

RUSTIC TART

Sommer Marsden

There's an old wooden sign in our bar that says NO WOODEN NICKELS. It was Duke's father's when he ran the bar. It's paddle shaped.

I became a rustic tart, meaning I married this man and moved to bumfuck nowhere, about three years ago.

On Friday nights the local boys get rowdy. Sometimes they fight, sometimes they tip cows, sometimes they just sing really loud and come as close to kissing each other in drunken stupors as rednecks can get. It's fun to watch.

On nights like tonight, I get a mind to do some rabble-rousing of my own.

Duke pours a draft for Farmer Stan. Farmer Stan has four teeth and smokes cherry-flavored cigars.

"Shitty pour," I say as I take the draft.

Duke's dark eyes flash at me, and I see that muscle in his forearm twitch.

Once I told him my self-imposed nickname, Rustic Tart, he's taken to calling me that. Occasionally. Only with provocation.

"Here you go, Stan. This one's on the house. Shitty pour."

Stan looks startled and Duke looks clenchy and I just smile.

He mixes a rum and cola for the new kid in town— Brad. Brad came here to raise soybeans. We sort of roll our eyes at him when he waxes poetic about how they're the wave of the future. They were the wave of the future ages ago.

I hold the drink up. "Looks weak to me."

That muscle in his forearm twitches again, and his eyes flit to the sign. It's quarter to two and the bar has stragglers.

I hand Brad the drink. "On the house." Then real loud: "Last call, y'all! Last call for alcohol."

I personally never drink on the job. Neither does Duke. We're sober as nuns.

And my stomach is thrumming with nervous energy. My whole body feels hot. My brain ablaze. I see Duke watching me and my face heats with blood. I have provoked. Now to see what happens.

He shuffles our stragglers out at two. Locks the door. Says nothing.

I'm biting my lip, trying not to let on that my entire

being is sizzling with anxiety. I clean the tables as he pulls the big green blinds down in front.

"Come here, Rosie."

My feet don't seem to want to move, but I force them. I haul the plastic bin of glasses to the bar. "What?" My tone is cocky. I'm shocked. I expect my voice to shiver the way I am.

"Get over here. You know what."

"Duke—"

"Hush up, Rustic Tart." He almost smiles at me. Almost. "Get that ass on this side of the bar."

The bar pads squish beneath my feet. The smell of beer and booze is cloying. I come to him and he grabs me up in one big arm and turns me. Plants my hands on the bar. I hear the paddle clack as he snatches it off the wall.

I brace myself but am shocked when he pulls my leggings down and then my underwear. They snag on my sneakers. He gets them off and uses them to twist around my wrists and then drapes my wrists over the taps.

"Shitty pour." He says it with the first blow. The wood is cool, smooth.

Warm swirling pleasure weaves itself in with my pain. I grunt when the blow lands and sigh when he pushes a thick finger inside me.

"Skimping," he says with the next. The thudding land of wood against flesh jars me all the way up to my teeth.

"Sorry," I gasp.

I get four more blows and he says nothing. I only hear the sound of his exertion and his rough breath as his arousal grows. He rubs his cock against my ass. He's hard and I wish his jeans would disappear. In a moment they do and he's pressed against me. Bare and hot. He spreads me, spears me, fucks me until my toes are barely touching the wet bar pads.

Just before Duke comes he finds my clit, pinches, rubs, strokes and I am coming with him. Shoulders aching from immobility. My head on the bar, my body quaking. Just another Friday night in bumfuck nowhere.

SPECIAL ORDER

Stella Harris

Model 156 waited impatiently for the plastic sheeting to be torn from her face and body; it was tight and restrictive. She couldn't see clearly through it and although she didn't need to breath, having her mouth and nose covered gave her a sense of unease. She wanted to see what her owner looked like, what kind of man he would be. She had no idea what to expect or what to hope for—the only men she'd seen were those at the factory where she'd been made, and she wasn't sure what would make one man better than another.

A door slammed and keys dropped onto a table. "Finally!" someone exclaimed, and then Model 156 heard footsteps coming toward where she rested, propped in the corner of the room.

The hands she'd been waiting for began to tear at the

plastic and once her eyes were uncovered she could see the man she belonged to. She supposed he was handsome; his features were fairly symmetrical. But the smile she expected to see when he looked at her never came. Instead his eyes ran over her critically, examining every inch of her face and her body with great care.

He used his hands to turn her face this way and that, to lift her arms and spread her legs. The touch she had longed for, had hoped would be warm and caring, was cold and professional. He touched her with less interest than the men at the factory. Those men had joked about "testing the goods" as their fingers poked and prodded, but at least they'd touched her with passion.

The man stepped back and frowned at her. She didn't know what he'd expected, but obviously she wasn't it. She wanted to reach out, to beg him to give her a chance, but she couldn't move, couldn't speak. He turned and walked away and there was nothing she could do but watch him leave.

Model 156 sat and listened as he banged around in the other room. She tried to think of ways she could get his attention, or be more appealing, but she had nothing to offer but her blank stare and silent, slightly parted lips.

He returned moments later and sat at his desk, setting a plate of food next to his computer. He stared at his screen; smiling at one thing then frowning at another, never so much as turning to look at her. She could smell the salty meats and cheeses he snacked on, and knew her mouth would water if it could.

After what felt like hours he stood and stretched, and finally he turned to look at her again. He still appeared displeased but there was a measure of calculation in his gaze. He reached out, took her by the hand, and pulled her along behind him into the bedroom. Apparently she was getting the second chance she'd wanted.

Once she was lying on the bed he began to undress. She'd never seen a nude man before and didn't know what to expect. As she watched she saw that his body was different from her own in several interesting ways.

He joined her on the bed and explored her body again; he seemed to be testing her, trying to get a reaction. His fingers pinched one nipple and then the other, watching her face closely as if hoping for some response—a response she couldn't provide. She felt both pain and pleasure but was helpless to express either.

He seemed to get bored with these experiments and the next thing she knew he was pressing into her; creating a sensation she couldn't begin to describe. This was not what she had expected. As he lay above her grunting and thrusting his eyes were closed tight, perhaps imagining the more responsive partner he'd hoped for.

It was over almost as quickly as it had begun. He rolled off of her, turned to the other side of the bed and was snoring within moments. She had no choice but to lie there staring at the ceiling for the rest of the night.

The next morning he went about his business without giving her a second look. Model 156 wondered if she'd be left in bed all day. She supposed it wasn't any better or worse than sitting up in the other room had been.

When he finally came toward her he was on the phone. "This was a mistake, I'm sending it back." She heard the words and her heart sank. She'd failed.

Less than twenty-four hours after leaving she found herself back at the factory, left on the loading dock. The air was cold against her exposed skin and the wood of the pallet was abrasive. The plastic she'd longed to be rid of only hours before now provided her only comfort. She couldn't help but worry about what would happen next. Would she be sent out again to another buyer or was this the end for her?

As she lay there, waiting, she wondered how they processed damaged goods.

THE DREAM POLICE

Kristina Lloyd

Last night, I dreamed I got stopped for speeding.

I had to pull over onto the hard shoulder on a warm, windy day while the blue light parked up in front of me. The guy who got out looked like a regular beat bobby, not a traffic cop. He approached, all boxy vest and swagger, silvery-white strips glinting on his black uniform. I lowered my passenger window and peered across. The lettering on his vest read POLICE. I flicked on my hazards and a small red heart flashed on my dashboard, pulse ticking in fear. Cars on the motorway whooshed past, fields beyond them billowing into the distance like a bright green ocean. I felt so still, as if the world were spinning without me.

"Could I ask you to step out of the vehicle?" said the cop, and I complied, of course. The breeze whipped my dress around my shins and tugged strands of hair across my face. Being so close to all that dangerous traffic dizzied me. I might have been standing on a cliff edge, the abyss trying to tempt me into flying.

I went to join him on the passenger side.

"Turn around," he said. "Hands on the car where I can see them. Legs apart."

Again, I cooperated, staying silent while he gave me a thorough pat down. His touch was blunt and heavy, and when he tapped around my breasts, I had to bite my lip to stop myself from moaning.

"Hands behind your back," he said.

I did as told, hearing the scratch and clink of metal. He locked my wrists together with a pair of cuffs, a rigid stem holding my hands apart.

"Now turn around. Step away from the car."

I faced him, wishing I could tuck my wind-lashed hair behind my ears.

He raised his brows. "You any idea how fast you were going?"

I shrugged. "Seventy?"

"A hundred and three."

"Wow."

The radio in his vest crackled and chirped. I glanced at the patrol car ahead and saw his colleague in the passenger seat, elbow jutting as he watched us in the wing mirror.

"I'm sorry, officer," I said. "I didn't realize. Must've been daydreaming."

He gave me a steady look, tilting his head as if trying to read who I was. "This potentially means a lot of paperwork for me," he said. "And I hate paperwork, don't you?"

"Absolutely."

His eyes narrowed. "Thought so." He adjusted his flies. "On your knees. Now!"

His abruptness alarmed me but I figured I didn't have a choice if I were to avoid a ticket. So I lowered myself as gracefully as I could, wishing my car offered a better screen from the traffic. The ground was gritty beneath my knees and the cop's big boots gleamed in the sunlight.

He exposed his cock, a glistening, violet-tipped beast of a thing, and told me to suck it.

"No," I said. "Officer, no! I'll kneel for your forgiveness but that—"

He grabbed a hank of my hair, his cock tapping against my face as he forced me to look up at him. "I'm sorry, lady," he said, voice dripping with sarcasm. "But I thought I just heard you say 'no.' Let's try that again, shall we? Open your mouth and suck on this dick before I make you."

I shook my head, lips clamped together, stray lengths of hair fluttering across my face. I saw his partner adjust his wing mirror.

"Okay, let's do it the hard way." The cop released my hair then pinched my nostrils between thumb and forefinger.

I began to count. I reached seven then, feeling flushed and panicky, I gave up. I gasped for air and the cop seized his chance to insert himself into my mouth, freeing my nostrils.

He moved with a slow, deliberate pace. "See? That's not too bad, is it?"

I looked up at him, coughing around his shaft. He altered his stance, knees slightly bent, feet apart. Again, he grabbed a fistful of hair, making my scalp sting. "That's right," he drawled, hips lunging. "You take it, speedy lady." His cock thrust faster. Cars roared past us, colors blurring into streaks on the edge of my vision.

"Take it!" he growled. "All of it. That's right. Make it disappear, girl. Go on! Every big, fat inch. It's all for you!"

The more excited he got, the worse he treated me. The worse he treated me, the more excited I got. I was a flood between my thighs, and my mouth was a mess of gasps, gagging, spillage and irritating wisps of hair. Then the censorious voices began crowding in: it was wrong for a woman to be kneeling before a brute; wrong for her to dream of being topped by a guy. Wrong, wrong, wrong! I was a traitor to my sex. A disgrace, a letdown. Ought to be ashamed.

"You like this, huh?" He gripped bunches of hair either side of my head, cock banging at my throat. "So what? You think I fucking care if you like it?"

Moments later, he flung back his head with a roar. Then he stared at my face, pumping out his groans, eyes popping as he spurted silky ribbons of whiteness into the darkness of my body. I swallowed him.

A pause. Even the cars seemed to go quiet. His shoulders sagged as he withdrew, tucking himself away, laughing lightly. He tasted bitter in my throat. The slam of a car door made my heart shoot. I turned, my hair rippling across my face. The cop's partner was striding toward us, smirking, a hand on the baton by his side. The breeze didn't touch these guys. They were rock. I was grass.

I wriggled and protested but the handcuffs kept me helpless.

"She's all yours," said cop number one, gesturing to me.

But I'm going too fast. It's my tendency. I need to pause it right there.

Cop number two is tonight's dream.

M

Alison Tyler

In the room, he walked all around me. I stood entirely still in my white fishnets, white attire. I might have felt virginal, except for the fact that my panties were dripping. The whole ride up in the elevator, I had sucked his cock while he'd stroked my hair and told me that I was thirteen minutes late.

Lucky number thirteen.

Now, I found myself trembling while I waited for him to make a move.

"I don't like waiting," he said.

I looked at the carpet, goldenrod, short but soft beneath my stockinged toes.

"Waiting makes me angry, and I don't like feeling angry."

He had never been a dom before, he'd written to me.

But something in my words made him think he could tame me. I'd had a dom before—oh, yes, I had. And the end of that relationship had left me in turmoil. For two years, I'd wandered, wondered, told myself I could go back to life before BDSM. Before kink in the morning. Pain-tinged pleasure in the evening. A word over the phone that would make me sit up straighter, that would make me cross my legs under my desk and pray for 5:00 p.m. to arrive.

My friends had advised me that relationships take healing time. They had no idea what I was mourning. Not the man, so much, but the excitement. The feeling of being alive. I'd been on hold for two years. I'd been a shadow, a black-and-white flicker of celluloid in an old-fashioned movie. My movements jerky. My behavior slightly slowed down. Drugged.

I'd placed the ad in a moment of desperation.

Many men had responded. D was the one I chose. He circled me now, a predator coming closer, and he said, "What does bondage do for you?"

I kept the smile from my face. I'd learned that much over time. "You don't get to know that yet." He seemed prepared for this response. He sat on the edge of the bed and motioned for me to come closer. He bent me over his lap and lifted my skirt. "You were going to get twenty," he said. "There will be an extra thirteen at the end. With my belt."

He gave me a perfect over-the-knee spanking that had me writhing and grinding against his knee. I had spanked myself over the past twenty-four months, to no satisfaction. I hadn't pulled back at the end, hadn't muffled the blows. And still I knew I was faking.

He didn't fake. He spanked me hard. And then he pushed me onto the bed, told me to strip and let me watch while he so slowly removed his belt from his slacks. It was enough to make me beg. *Go faster. I've been waiting so long. Do me harder. Do me now.* But I couldn't. I knew my place. I steeled my body. I waited.

He struck the first blow, and I sighed. The second landed, and I moaned. He gripped my hair in his hand, pulled my head back and said, "Why?"

"It wakes me up," I said.

He landed a third blow, crisscrossing the first two.

"You sleepwalk?"

"Through life," I told him, as I realized the words were true. Without this—the pain and the pleasure, the bondage and the dominance, the B-D-S-M, I was one more vanilla cupcake in the bakery window, breath-steamed glass of desire fogging up the vision.

I could see his hard-on through his slacks. I knew he hadn't come yet, had simply allowed himself to enjoy the warm wet bliss of my mouth in the elevator. He struck me again, twice more, and then he pulled a pair of cuffs from his pocket. Slim leather cuffs that he buckled on my wrists, stretching me out. "We'll get the toys," he said, "the devices. I'll keep you locked by my side at night. I'll make you wear a butt plug. A ball gag. I'll give you everything you need."

He landed the belt in between the words, and I rocked my hips on the mattress and I wept against the pillows.

Not from the pain, you understand. But from the relief.

ABOUT
THE EDITOR

Called "a trollop with a laptop" by *East Bay Express,* "a literary siren" by Good Vibrations and "the mistress of literary erotica" by Violet Blue, **ALISON TYLER** is naughty and she knows it.

Over the past two decades, Ms. Tyler has written more than twenty-five explicit novels, including *Tiffany Twisted, Melt with You* and *The ESP Affair.* Her novels and short stories have been translated into Japanese, Dutch, German, Italian, Norwegian, Spanish and Greek. When not writing sultry short stories, she edits erotic anthologies, including *Alison's Wonderland*, *Kiss My Ass*, *Skirting the Issue* and *Torn.*

Ms. Tyler is loyal to coffee (black), lipstick (red), and tequila (straight). She has tattoos, but no piercings; a wicked tongue, but a quick smile; and bittersweet memories, but no regrets. She believes it won't rain if she doesn't bring an umbrella, prefers hot and dry to cold and wet, and loves to spout her favorite motto: You can sleep when you're dead. She chooses Led Zeppelin over the Beatles, the Cure over NIN and the Stones over everyone. Yet although she appreciates good rock, she has a pitiful weakness for '80s hair bands.

In all things important, she remains faithful to her partner of nearly twenty years, but she still can't choose just one perfume.